FORBIDDEN FRIENDS

Anne-Marie Conway

GALAXY

PLUS

First published in Great Britain in 2013
by Usborne Publishing Ltd
This Large Print edition published 2013
by AudioGO Ltd
by arrangement with
Usborne Publishing Ltd

ISBN: 978 1471 359798

British Library Cataloguing in Publication Data available

Printed and bound in Great Britain by
TJ International Limited

For Julia—BFF—through good times and bad! xxx

Bee

The policeman came round early this morning, just before eight. It was awful. I had to sit in the living room and answer loads of questions about Dad. Did I know where he was? Did he say anything to me before he left? Did I remember anything that had seemed out of the ordinary? Nan sat next to me on the sofa, holding my hand as tight as she could, but it didn't help. My stomach was in knots. I didn't have a clue where Dad was. I hadn't seen him since Friday after school, and that was three days ago.

'Don't worry, Bee,' the policeman kept saying, 'you're not in any trouble. No one's cross with you. But if there's anything at all you remember...'

Mum came in, carrying a tray of tea and biscuits. She looked dreadful. Lank hair, no make-up, dark shadows under her eyes.

'Something's happened to him,' she muttered. 'I mean, where *is* he? How can someone just disappear into thin air?'

She tried to add sugar to the mugs but her hand was trembling so badly it spilled over the tray. I snuggled in to Nan, trying not to cry.

'Here, Val, let me,' said Nan, reaching out to take the spoon from her. 'Everything's going to be fine. You don't want to go upsetting Bee.'

But Mum stared right through her, swaying from side to side as if she was about to pass out. I don't think she'd even noticed I was there. She's usually so calm and in control but it was as if someone had hypnotized her. I felt like giving her a shake or

1

clicking my fingers in front of her face, just to wake her up, but the policeman still had lots of questions for me.

He wanted to know if Mum and Dad had been rowing or if Dad had ever gone missing before; maybe stayed at a mate's house after a night out, that sort of thing. He even asked if I thought Dad might be seeing someone else. He didn't use those words exactly, but I knew that was what he was getting at. I nearly died of embarrassment. My dad's the last person on earth who would ever go off with another woman—he's just not like that. He doesn't come out of his study long enough to *meet* anyone, let alone run off with them. But the truth was, Mum and Dad *had* been arguing a lot before he disappeared.

I glanced at Mum. She hadn't said anything to the policeman about the rows when he asked her so I wasn't sure if I should mention them.

It all started when this letter arrived for Mum a couple of weeks ago. It was in a pale pink envelope and I remember thinking it must be an invitation or something. Mum opened it when she got in from work, at the table, while we were all having dinner.

I watched her face change as she read it. First it sort of froze, then she blinked a few times, frowning. She glanced up at Dad, and then looked back down at the letter, her eyes filling with tears. I was about to ask her who it was from, but before I could say anything she leaped up from the table and ran out of the room and a moment later Dad jumped up and followed her.

I heard them shouting upstairs—well, Mum was shouting and Dad just kept saying no, and that he

2

wasn't willing to do it. At one point I heard him say that Mum was mad to even *consider it* after so much time had passed. I had no idea what was in the letter or what he wasn't 'willing to do' but they carried on rowing about it for days. Mum begged him to reconsider and in the end she was so upset she made him sleep on the sofa.

It was awful; I'd never seen her so angry. They hardly ever row, and when they do it never drags on for more than a day at most. I was desperate to know who the letter was from and what was going on, but they wouldn't tell me. They said it was private; something they had to sort out for themselves.

I was still struggling to decide what I should tell the policeman. But I had to say something, so I just told him that I'd last seen Dad on Friday afternoon when I'd come in from school and that I hadn't noticed anything strange about his behaviour. I hardly talk to him these days anyway, not properly. We used to be really close; I used to tell him everything, but not any more. And the truth was I'd been distracted on Friday. I hadn't been paying much attention to Dad. I'd had other things on my mind.

It was the last day of the summer term and I'd just survived my first year at Glendale High. Melissa Knight and some of her pathetic mates had followed me out of school and down the road to the bus stop, calling out and laughing as I hurried ahead of them. Taunting me every step of the way with their nasty jokes and mean comments.

I kept my head down, praying the bus would arrive before they caught up with me. I had a horrible feeling I'd left half my stuff at school, but I didn't dare go back. I knew Mum would flip when she found out, especially if I'd forgotten my trainers. She was always going on about how expensive everything was and how much everything cost to replace, but what was I supposed to do?

Melissa Knight had been on my case from the moment I started at Glendale High. It was just 'looks' to begin with—rolling her eyes and smirking—and snorting when I said anything in class. Then it was names: 'Bookworm Bee' and 'Brainiac Bee' and other stupid things like that. But the last few weeks of term she'd been pushing me around, threatening me, following me out of school. I didn't fit in and she knew it.

In the end, I ran all the way back home without waiting for the bus. They were miles away by then but I could still hear their voices in my head as I raced down the street to our house and burst through the front door. Dad was in the kitchen making a sandwich. I remember *that* much. It was cheese and tomato. He looked up as I came in.

'Oh, hi, Bee.'

'Hi.' I dropped my bag and shrugged off my school cardie, bending over to catch my breath.

'Good day?'

I bit my lip. 'Yeah, I guess.' I wanted to tell him about Melissa Knight. I wanted to tell him so much it made my tummy hurt. But I couldn't.

'Shall I make you a sandwich? I've been upstairs working all day and I suddenly realized how hungry I was.'

'No thanks. What time's Mum coming home?'

He started to answer, to tell me he wasn't sure— of course he wasn't, they weren't even speaking— but then he stopped suddenly, mid-sentence. There were some tickets propped up against the toaster. They looked like airline tickets. He stared at them for a moment and then without saying another word, he turned and walked out of the room.

I wasn't sure whether to tell the policeman about the tickets or not, and I was still wondering whether I should mention the rows and the fact that Dad had been sleeping downstairs. It all felt so private—not exactly something you chat about with a stranger. But that wasn't the only thing stopping me. There was also the way Dad's face changed when he first saw the tickets. He'd looked frightened. Just for a split second. Well, I think it was fear, but if only I'd been paying more attention...

The policeman was staring at me, waiting for me to tell him more. He probably thought Dad had gone off with another woman anyway. I sat there, picking at the ragged skin around my thumbnail. I hadn't actually seen Dad again after he walked out of the kitchen. He went upstairs and then a few minutes later he came back down and I heard the front door slam. No goodbye or anything. It was as if he'd suddenly remembered he had to be somewhere very important.

I didn't think much of it at the time. I didn't even bother to look at the tickets. I just assumed they were to do with Mum's work, and anyway I was pleased to have the house to myself. It was only later, when Mum came home, that I started to feel uneasy. It was late by then and when I told her Dad had left without saying goodbye she tried calling him, but his phone was switched off.

She must've called him about fifty times after that, getting more and more agitated as the evening wore on. I asked her about the tickets then—about what they were for, why she'd left them propped up against the toaster like that and why Dad had walked out when he saw them—but she said she'd explain everything when Dad was home. By the time I went to bed I was really scared. I'd started to imagine all sorts of terrible things. It was so unlike Dad to disappear. No phone call or text message. Nothing.

I looked across at Mum now. She was still standing in the middle of the room, staring off into the distance. It was beginning to freak me out. There had to be something we could do. I tried to remember more details about the tickets—anything at all that might help us find Dad. If only I'd bothered to look at them properly when I'd had the chance.

The policeman cleared his throat. He was still waiting for me to say something. He looked bored, as if he wanted to finish up and get away.

'Well, there were these tickets,' I said softly. I didn't really want Mum to hear but I couldn't keep quiet any longer.

He sat up a bit straighter. 'Tickets? What sort of tickets, Bee? Can you explain?'

I leaned forward, ready to tell him, but just at that moment Mum's phone rang. She snapped out of her trance, lurching towards the table to grab it.

'*Phillip? Is that you?*' Then she looked up at us, smiling, her eyes filling with tears. 'It's him,' she told us, sinking down onto the couch. 'Where *are* you? I've been so worried!'

My eyes filled with tears too. I was just so relieved. Mum was quiet for a moment, listening to Dad. 'I can't talk about that right now,' she hissed, glancing at the policeman and then turning her shoulder slightly. 'You've got no right to say that! It's not your decision to make—this is something that affects all of us.' The policeman stood up, watching Mum closely, but she turned right round and moved towards the hallway so he couldn't hear. The conversation with Dad lasted another minute or so and then she closed her phone, her lips set in a thin, straight line.

'Is everything okay, Mrs. Brooks?' the policeman asked.

'Yes, fine. Everything's fine,' she said. 'I'm so sorry. He's fine. We didn't mean to waste your time. I was just...you know...I was just so worried.'

The policeman waved his hand. 'No, you were right to call. Best to be on the safe side. I'll have to fill out a report, so if you could just help me with a few last details...' He sat back down, taking an official-looking form out of his bag. Then there were more endless questions—it seemed to go on and on, and I began to wonder if he'd ever go.

'Thank you so much,' said Nan, when he'd finished. 'We really appreciate you coming round. It's just so out of character, you see.' She led him out to the front door, chatting on about Dad and how reliable he usually is and how he'd never done anything like this before.

As soon as they were out of the living room, I turned to face Mum on the couch. 'Where is he? Is he okay?'

Mum took hold of my hands, but she couldn't quite meet my eyes. 'He's fine,' she said brightly. 'He's gone to stay at Uncle Ron's for a little while. It won't be for long.'

Uncle Ron is Dad's brother, but they've never

7

been close. We usually only see him at Christmas. My heart started to thump in my chest. 'Are you and Dad breaking up? Is that why he's there?'

'No, it's nothing like that,' she said, smoothing my hair away from my face. 'Look, why don't you go back to bed, Bee? You must be exhausted. We all are. I really don't want you to worry about any of this. Come on, I'll take you up.'

She was trying to reassure me, but I shook my head. I didn't want to go to bed. I wanted to know why Dad had been at Uncle Ron's for three days without calling us and what it was about those tickets that had made him leave in such a hurry. Just then, Nan came back in from seeing the policeman out.

'So where is he, Val?'

'He's gone to stay at Ron's for a few days,' said Mum. Her eyes darted from Nan to me and then back to Nan. She obviously didn't want to say anything else while I was in the room.

'Be a good girl, Bee. Make us a fresh pot of tea, would you, darling?' said Nan, taking the hint from Mum. They were trying to get rid of me so they could talk. It was so frustrating.

'But I want to know what's going on as well. I'm not a baby!'

Nan smiled. 'Of course you're not, and we'll have a good chat about everything as soon as you've made the tea, won't we, Val?' Mum nodded vaguely, but I was sure she had no intention of telling me anything. She'd been really secretive over the past few weeks, ever since the mysterious letter and the row with Dad. Nan handed me the tea tray. 'Go on, darling. We'll wait for you, promise.'

They started talking as soon as I left the room. They were whispering but I could still make out some of what they were saying. Mum was talking about the letter. She said Dad didn't believe she'd go through with it until he saw the tickets. I couldn't hear what Nan said back. Something about panicking and the truth, but her voice was muffled, as if she'd put her hand over her mouth.

I trailed into the kitchen and flipped the switch on the kettle. I couldn't quite believe any of this had actually happened: the letter, the row, Dad disappearing and the policeman coming round. Nan was right when she'd said it was out of character. Nothing *ever* happens around here. We're just the boring Brooks family. The knot in my stomach pulled tighter. I was so relieved that Dad was okay...I just wished that I could rewind the clock to Friday and hide those tickets before he ever saw them.

I took the tea back in, determined to get some answers.

'There she is,' said Mum. She was still trying to pretend everything was normal, but her voice was so brittle it sounded as if it might crack into a million pieces.

'This isn't funny any more!' I burst out. 'Can one of you please tell me what's going on!' I was beginning to feel really anxious. I'd tried not to let the thought enter my head but maybe the policeman had been right. Except maybe it was *Mum*, not Dad, who was seeing someone else, some other man, and the letter had been from him. Maybe Mum and Dad were splitting up and they didn't know how to tell me. I looked over at Nan. 'Please, Nan, you promised. Just tell me.'

9

And that's when Nan said the strangest thing of all.

'We need to pop out and buy you a new suitcase, Bee, my love, because first thing Saturday morning we're all going to Spain.'

Lizzie

Boring, boring, boring! It was Friday. My worst day of the week. Double literacy followed by French.

'I've got to go out for a little while, Lizzie. I won't be long.' Dad reached across the kitchen table for his car keys. 'I want you to read this article on climate change and then answer the questions on the last page.' He stopped at the door. 'And remember to use full sentences. I don't want any sloppy work.'

'Not comprehension *again*, Dad! We've already done three this week. Can't we do something else, *please*?'

He breathed in through his nose, closing his eyes, as if he was trying to stay calm. 'We've actually done it twice, and that's precisely because you're still not answering the questions properly. Full sentences or we'll be doing another one this afternoon. Do you understand?'

Yes, Dad. No, Dad. Three bags full, Dad!

I *hate* literacy. No, let me be more precise: I LOVE reading and writing, but I HATE doing comprehension. I'd be happy to read all day long if only Dad would let me, but he's in charge of the curriculum. He's the one who makes all the rules

10

around here and what *I* want doesn't come into it.

I've been homeschooled ever since I was four, and I'm nearly thirteen now. No one ever bothered to ask me if I wanted to go to a proper school; it's not like I had a *choice*. I didn't even know what a school was back then. I thought *going to school* was something that happened in stories and that ordinary children like me had their lessons at home—I thought it was normal.

It wasn't that bad to start with. The two boys who live at the end of our street, Dilan and Danesh, came over every day, and Mum taught all three of us together. Danesh is the same age as me and Dilan is about a year and a half older. I don't think we ever did any proper lessons, we just had the coolest time playing with Play-Doh and building dens and running wild in the garden.

Danesh was always very shy and quiet—he was the serious one—but it was Dilan I really liked. He used to hide behind Dad, pulling silly faces to make us laugh. He taught me how to slide down the stairs inside my duvet cover and how to trick Mum into giving us extra sweets after lunch. We were a little gang and he made every day seem like an adventure.

I remember once Mum helped us to make this amazing papier-mâché dragon. I was in charge of the tail, Danesh did the body and Dilan made the head. He painted table-tennis balls orange for the eyes and made teeth out of white polystyrene. When it was finished we somehow squashed up right inside the dragon, all three of us, and roared whenever Mum came in the room. Even now, if I close my eyes tight and concentrate really hard, I can smell the glue and the paint and Dilan's hot

11

breath on my face.

But then one day Dilan and Danesh stopped coming round. It was just after my seventh birthday. Mum said they'd started at Merryfields, the local primary school, and that Dad was going to take over my lessons from then on. Apparently his web design company was so successful that he could put someone else in charge of the day-to-day running of the office, while Mum took care of any extra admin from home.

It was a total nightmare. He gave me this big speech about how the time to play was over. My lessons became far more serious after that. I was never allowed to go out in the garden, or do any of the other things I loved so much—it was just maths and science and French and Spanish and lots and lots of BORING comprehension.

I skimmed through the article on climate change. I was good at skimming. The answers were always so obvious anyway. They were right there in the text, so what on earth was the point of writing them down all over again?

The ozone layer is important because it stops too many of the sun's ultraviolet rays getting through to Earth.

1. Why is the ozone layer important?

The ozone layer is important because it stops too many of the sun's ultraviolet rays getting through to Earth.

I dropped my pencil in despair. I didn't care about the stupid ozone layer. It was such a beautiful day, the last thing I wanted was to waste the whole morning cooped up inside, answering questions on climate change. I wanted to ditch the comprehension and hang about outside until I caught a glimpse of Dilan. He pretty much ignores me these days. He doesn't remember the cookies and the dens and being squashed inside the dragon.

I was about halfway through when Mum came in to make a cup of tea. She peered over my shoulder to see how I was getting on.

'Can't I have a break, Mum, *please*? Dad's popped out for a bit and I'm *soooo* bored.'

'Best not, Lizzie,' she said, her eyes darting towards the door. 'He might be back any minute and he won't be happy if you're not working. I want you to get finished anyway so you can go up and start packing.'

Packing. My heart sank right down to my trainers. I didn't want to pack. Not for Spain. The tickets had been stuck up on the fridge for weeks. Mum had booked them online and printed them straight off. She didn't need to tell me where we were going anyway. It was the same every year. Same dates, same place, same miserable holiday.

'Can't we go somewhere else this year, just for once? I'm so sick of going to Spain.' The words were out of my mouth before I could stop them.

Mum swung round. 'What do you mean?' she said, her face flushing very red suddenly. 'How can you even ask something like that?'

I stared down at my books. 'I don't know, I was just thinking it would be nice to go somewhere different…just for a change…I mean would Luke even *want* us to go back there year after year…' I trailed off.

Mum didn't say anything for a moment. She opened and closed her mouth but nothing came out. My words hung between us, swelling to fill the awful silence.

'Go to your room, Lizzie.'

My head snapped up. It was Dad. He'd come back in and was standing by the door, his face hard and angry.

'I'm sorry. I...I didn't mean it. I don't even know why I said it.'

Mum turned away from us to face the sink, her shoulders hunched up to her ears. I really *was* sorry; I hadn't meant to upset her—I was just so frustrated I couldn't help myself.

'*Up to your room!*' Dad roared, taking a step towards me. '*How dare you talk about Luke like that? As if you know! As if you know anything!*'

I leaped up and pushed past him, running out of the kitchen and up the stairs to my room. I hate it when Dad loses his temper. It's not the shouting so much; I'm used to that by now. It's more the way he looks at me—actually, straight *through* me, as if I don't exist, his eyes like ice-cold shards of glass. I'll bet you anything he never looked at Luke like that. I'll bet you anything Luke never got the shouting *or* the ice-cold eyes.

Luke was my big brother. He died in an accident just before my third birthday, but sometimes it feels as if he never died at all. I don't actually remember what life was like before he died; I was too young. But the fact that he's not here any more, the fact that he's *gone*, somehow seems to take up more space in our house than if he was still around.

There are pictures of him on nearly every wall. Luke when he was a baby. Luke on his first day

14

at school. Luke on a beach somewhere, eating a strawberry ice cream. I've been staring at those photos for so many years I know them off by heart. I know his shiny smile, and bright blue eyes, his perfect blond hair, but I don't really *know* him. I don't know his voice or his laugh or the way he used to walk. He's been smiling down at me for as long as I can remember, but as far as I'm concerned he could be anyone.

I sat on my bed, writing my diary, pouring all my anger out onto the pages. I tell my diary everything. All my hopes and dreams, as well as all the things I hate about my life—like being homeschooled, stuck in the house with Dad all day, totally trapped. It's the only place I can say what I really feel without upsetting everyone or getting into trouble.

I was still writing when Mum snuck up to see me. She ducked into the room carrying a cup of tea and some toast.

'I'm sorry, Lizzie. Dad didn't mean it. He'll calm down in a bit.'

I slipped my diary under my pillow and turned to the wall, tears prickling at the corners of my eyes. Mum was always apologizing for Dad, making excuses, but she never stuck up for me when it mattered. I didn't realize that when I was younger—I thought she was my ally against Dad. But the older I got, the more I realized that she was just trying to pacify him, keep him calm—that she wasn't really on my side at all.

'I've brought you some toast and—'

'I don't want any stupid toast!'

'Look, it's just a sensitive time right now,' she went on, putting the tray down on my dressing table and coming over to perch on the edge of my bed. 'You know the anniversary is coming up...'

'Okay, I'm sorry, but I still don't want to go to Spain again this year. It's not a crime, is it? I just wish we could be normal. I wish I could go to school and have friends round, ordinary stuff like that.'

'You do have friends round, Lizzie.'

'Yes, but only girls that have been hand-picked and approved by Dad. His friends' children. It's so unfair. I'm nearly thirteen—I should be allowed to make my own friends. It's like living in a prison.'

Mum sighed. 'Just let him get through the summer, through the anniversary, and I'm sure things will settle down. He doesn't mean to get so worked up. He never used to lose his temper before Luke...' She broke off, her eyes filling with tears.

Luke again. It was ALWAYS about Luke.

'It doesn't matter,' I muttered. I can't stand it when she cries. 'At least I got out of doing that boring comprehension.'

'Come on, I'll help you pack if you want,' she said, doing her best to smile. 'Dad's popped up to the library to get you some books out for the holiday. He's not actually coming with us for the first week, so it'll just be the two of us.'

My head snapped up. *A whole week away without Dad?* 'Are you serious?'

Mum nodded. 'He's got some important things to sort out at the office. Work stuff. He'll meet us out there in time for the anniversary.'

Luke died during our first-ever family holiday

16

to Spain, so this year—the tenth anniversary—was going to be even worse than usual. I'd have to tiptoe around, watch everything I said. Mum was desperate for me to miss Luke, for the anniversary to mean as much to me as it did to them. But how are you supposed to miss someone you don't even remember?

Bee

S*pain?* I honestly thought Nan was joking at first.

'What do you mean?' I said weakly, convinced it was a wind-up. 'We can't go to Spain.' I mean apart from the fact that Dad was at Uncle Ron's and the police had just been round, we didn't actually *do* holidays in our family. Mum was always too busy working and Dad never came out of his office long enough to *book* a holiday, let alone go on one. I couldn't remember the last time I'd stayed overnight anywhere, apart from on my Year Six school trip to the Isle of Wight.

'I know it's a bit out of the blue,' Nan cut in, 'but we all need a break, Bee, especially your mum.'

'But what about Dad? How can you even think about going on holiday when Dad's not here? And you haven't told me when he's coming home. You haven't told me *anything*.'

'He says he doesn't want to come on holiday with us, he's too busy,' said Mum, her voice just as brittle as before. She didn't exactly look as if she was in the mood for a holiday herself. And how did she know Dad didn't want to come? Was that what he'd been saying on the phone? Was that why

17

he'd walked out when he saw the tickets? I was beginning to feel as if I was still asleep, trapped inside a terrible dream.

'When did you actually plan this trip? I mean, first Dad goes missing, then he calls to say he's staying at Uncle Ron's, and now you tell me we're going to Spain. None of it makes any sense.'

'I booked the holiday at the beginning of last week,' said Nan. 'Your mum's already arranged the time off work. To tell you the truth, Bee, it was supposed to be a surprise for you. Two weeks at the Costa de las Cuevas resort.'

'But what about Dad's ticket?' I said, my voice rising. 'I don't want to go unless he comes with us! It doesn't feel right! And if it was supposed to be a surprise, why did Mum leave the tickets out like that?'

'I left them out for Dad to see in the morning,' said Mum. 'I didn't realize they'd still be there when you got in from school. Come on, Bee, it's just a holiday. You'll love it once we get there.'

Nan nodded, agreeing. 'Don't worry about your dad; he's happy for the three of us to go on our own.'

I shook my head, more confused than ever, but I couldn't help feeling a tiny flicker of excitement. I hadn't been on a proper holiday for years. The girls at school were always going off on exotic holidays, boasting about all the amazing places they'd visited. I could only imagine what it would be like to climb the Eiffel Tower or go to Disneyland or lie on a sun-drenched beach somewhere.

Nan started to describe the little hotel where we'd be staying. She said I'd be able to swim in the sea and learn how to waterski and eat loads of

18

paella. Mum just sat there, zoned out again. It was obvious she was still worried about Dad and she wasn't the only one. I wanted to know how they were ever going to make up if he was at Uncle Ron's and we were hundreds of miles away in Spain.

*   *   *

It still seemed unreal the next day. I could hardly believe it was true; that we were actually going on holiday to Spain. Nan and I went up to the High Road to buy my new suitcase and when we got back I went round to see my next-door neighbour, Bailey. His older sister, Carin, let me in and I raced up the stairs to his room, two at a time, desperate to tell him what was going on.

'*Spain!*' he said. 'Blimey, Bee, it's alright for some!' He was on the floor, attempting to wrestle a sleeping bag into his old school backpack, rolling around as if he was grappling with a crocodile. 'I thought your mum and dad never had time for holidays abroad?'

'They don't usually, they always say they haven't got the money, but you know what my nan's like once she gets an idea in her head. It was supposed to be a surprise or something. And anyway, it's just me, Mum and Nan.' I hesitated for a moment. 'My dad's not coming; he's gone to stay at my Uncle Ron's for a bit.'

Bailey glanced up. 'What is it, ladies only?'

'Something like that,' I said. 'Except my mum won't tell me what's really going on.'

'What do you mean?'

'Well, they had this massive fight and then my

19

dad left the house after I got home on Friday and we didn't even know where he was until yesterday morning.'

'Why didn't you tell me?' said Bailey.

'I was going to, but I kept hoping he'd show up suddenly. The police came round and everything.' My tummy clenched up. It sounded even worse saying it out loud.

'The *police*?' said Bailey. 'No way! My mum's always storming off when she rows with my dad but it's never been as serious as that. Look on the bright side though...' He glanced up at me from the floor. 'This time next week you'll be soaking up the rays, while I'm stuck in the middle of some muddy field in the pouring rain. Hey, I bet you've never even been on a plane before.'

'I have, but it was so long ago I can't actually remember. What's it like?'

'Noisy,' he said. 'Especially take-off. And boring. But Spain's not that far, a couple of hours max.'

I've lived next door to Bailey since I was five and he was six. We've grown up together, more like brother and sister than neighbours, I guess. My real brother Aidan left home years ago, first chance he got, and I hardly see him these days. I used to wish Bailey *was* my brother. He was always moaning about his family, but I'd have swapped them with mine any day.

'Hey, give me a hand with this, would you?' he said, as the sleeping bag sprang out of his backpack again, landing in a heap at his feet. 'I'll be here till Christmas at this rate and we're supposed to be...' He stopped mid-sentence as he stared up at me, confusion spreading across his face.

'You look different, Bee.'

'No I don't.'

He nodded slowly, as if he was working out the answer to some incredibly complicated puzzle. I could feel myself turning crimson. I hate it when he stares at me like that.

'Yes you do. It's your hair, isn't it? You've done something different to your hair!'

'No I haven't, don't be stupid,' I said, pushing my hands through my uncontrollable mess of curls. I couldn't do anything different with my hair even if I wanted to. 'I…I…I'm just wearing a new top, that's all.'

I grabbed the sleeping bag and scrunched it up as small as I could, willing my face to cool down. Yes, I'd always thought of Bailey as a brother, but in the last few months things had started to become all mixed up and confused. It wasn't that I fancied him or anything; I just didn't feel as comfortable around him as I'd used to. And I'm sure he realized—the way I blushed like an idiot every time he even looked at me! At least that was one thing I wouldn't have to worry about while we were in Spain.

*   *   *

The next couple of days dragged by. It was awful being home without Dad. He texted me a few times to say he was fine and how lucky I was to be going to Spain. *All that lovely sunshine,* he wrote. *I'm so envious! xx* I was desperate for him to show up suddenly and say he'd changed his mind about coming with us, but he didn't even call. I tried calling him myself, but it went straight to voicemail every time.

21

I kept asking Mum if she'd seen him or spoken to him since Monday, and whether I could call him at Uncle Ron's myself, but it was impossible to get a straight answer out of her.

'I don't really want you bothering him right now, Bee,' she said, vaguely. It was the day before the holiday and she was sorting out a pile of washing. 'He just needs a bit of space to think things through. I know it's unsettling for you, but then Dad's never been a great one for going away, has he? It's hard enough to get him out of his study, let alone on a plane to another country.'

'Yes, but why is he staying at Uncle Ron's? And what is it he needs to think through?'

'It's just—'

'I know you're breaking up!' I interrupted, blurting out my worst fear. 'I wish you'd just *tell me*.'

'Of course we're not breaking up!' cried Mum. 'We're going through a little rough patch at the moment, but it's nothing like that!'

'Well, what is it then?' I said, desperate to understand.

But she just shook her head, sighing. 'It's complicated, Bee. I can't really talk about it right now; I've still got so much to sort out. We'll talk in Spain. I'll explain *everything*, I promise.'

She'd been promising to explain things ever since the letter arrived, but I was still waiting. I don't think she realized how confused I was—how weird it felt to be busy getting ready for a holiday without my dad.

'I just wish everything could go back to the way it was before that letter arrived and all the rows started,' I said, my eyes filling with tears. 'I hate

22

being here without Dad.'

Mum dropped the dress she was folding and pulled me into her arms. 'Hey, come on, Bee,' she said gently, tipping my chin up and wiping my eyes. 'I know it's difficult, I miss Dad as well, but everything will seem so much brighter once we're away.'

It was nice to have a cuddle. My mum's not usually the easiest person to talk to if you're worried about something. She always says there's a practical solution to every problem—but there are some problems that can't be fixed no matter how hard you try. She gave me another quick hug and then went back to the washing. 'Why don't you pop upstairs to pack and then when you've finished I'll make us both a nice cup of tea.'

I left her to it and trailed up to my room. My new suitcase from Nan was brilliant—really funky with bright pink and purple flowers all over it, and a handle that pulls out so you can wheel it along the ground. I took ages sorting everything out. I made little piles of clothes all over my bed and then arranged them in the case, layer by layer, with my books spread out on top.

I think I ended up with more books than clothes. It was just so difficult trying to decide which ones to take and which ones to leave behind. I put some school books in as well. We had a brilliant poetry topic to do over the holidays—we had to write a series of poems on any theme we liked, and then when we got back, Mrs. Wren, our literacy teacher, was going to publish them in a book for the school library.

I hadn't picked a theme for my poems yet but I decided to take a few poetry books in case I got any ideas while we were away. Two weeks of reading and writing by the sea sounded like my idea of heaven... If only Dad could be there to enjoy it with us. I checked my phone again to see if I'd missed a call from him or another text, but the only message I had was from Bailey, saying, *Stuck in a field, raining x.*

When I'd finished packing I hauled my suitcase downstairs and left it ready by the front door. I was pretty scared about the flight and mega scared about what was going on between Mum and Dad, but when I thought about Melissa Knight and school, there was a part of me that was desperate to leave for Spain right that minute.

*   *   *

It was packed at the airport. The queue to check in our cases moved quite quickly, but then we had to go through security. That took ages. Just when we finished at one desk, we had to move along and queue up at the next. They asked us lots of questions about liquids and creams and whether we understood all the rules and regulations. We weren't even allowed to take a bottle of water through with us.

Mum was fine to start off with but she seemed to grow more anxious with every question they asked her. She kept checking and rechecking the passports as if she was scared they might disappear, her hands shaking so badly at one point she could barely turn the pages. It was so unlike her.

As soon as we'd passed through all the checks, Nan sent her straight off to the bar.

'Get yourself a whisky or a brandy or something

to steady your nerves,' she said. 'Don't worry about us; I'll take Bee to buy a magazine.'

I linked arms with Nan, feeling happy for the first time in days. I was safe at the airport; far away from Glendale High. I hadn't told Mum and Dad or Nan about the bullying. They were all so excited when the letter came to say I'd been offered a place at Glendale; they said it was the proudest day of their lives. And I was just as excited as they were to begin with… But that was before I realized that a geeky scholarship girl like me—or a 'charity case' as Melissa likes to call me—was never going to stand a chance.

It was crazy to be so scared of someone, but every time Melissa looked at me, with that nasty sneer on her face as if she'd just stepped in something disgusting, my brain literally froze up. It was like an automatic response. Almost as if she was a GIANT and I was a tiny ant and all she had to do was put her foot out and squash me flat.

*   *   *

Bailey was right about take-off, it was really noisy. I held onto Nan's hand, digging my nails in as the plane tore down the runway, but as soon as we were up and through the clouds I began to relax. I pressed my nose to the window, watching the cars and houses and fields shrink below us until they looked like little plastic toys. I tried to work out where exactly in the sky you crossed from one country to another and relaxed even more when the pilot announced that we'd left England and were flying over the western tip of France.

Mum hardly said a word the entire time we

were in the air—she was just frozen in her seat like a waxwork. But as the plane touched down she suddenly came to life, grabbing hold of Nan's arm as she hauled herself up. 'I'm really not sure about this,' she said, as if we'd only gone five minutes up the road. 'I know what you're going to say, but I think maybe Phillip was right. I'm not ready. I can't face it.'

Nan steered her off the plane and towards the arrivals area, doing her best to calm Mum down. I followed behind, a sour feeling in my stomach. I wished I knew what was upsetting her so much, and what she meant when she said she wasn't ready. I knew there was no point asking her though—she'd never tell me. It was obviously something to do with Dad and coming away to Spain without him, but the way she was talking made it sound far more serious than that. It was as if they were breaking up for ever.

*   *   *

The airport was really small compared with the one in London, and flooded with light. I tried to read all the Spanish signs—it was one of the languages I was going to start learning at Glendale when I moved into Year Eight. *Bienvenido a España*—Welcome to Spain. And *Control de pasaportes*—This way to passport control. I hurried along, practising my accent, rolling the unfamiliar words around in my mouth.

We had to queue for a while at passport control, but as soon as we were through, Mum went to grab a trolley and Nan and I made our way over to the baggage reclaim area to find our luggage. It was easy as anything to spot mine amongst all the boring black and brown cases. I watched it trundle towards me around the baggage carousel, ready to grab it as it came past. I waited until it was just about level with where I was standing and then snaked my arm through the crowd of people in front of me, reaching for the handle.

I was sure I had it, I'd timed it just right, but at that exact same moment, a girl standing next to me thrust *her* arm out, grasped the handle and yanked the case off the belt.

'I'm really sorry, but that's mine,' I said, turning to face her, surprised. 'Look.' I showed her the label where I'd written my name in big, blue letters.

'Here you are then,' she said, letting go quickly. 'Only my case is exactly the same as yours.'

She turned back and a second later stretched her arm through the crowds again and pulled an identical suitcase off the carousel. She held it up to show to me, as if she was worried I might not believe her, and then set it down, striding off towards the exit as if she'd been travelling the world for years and knew exactly where she was going.

Lizzie

Mum didn't mention the *anniversary* again until we were at the airport. We'd found a quiet cafe away from all the crowds while we waited for our flight to be called. I could tell she wanted to talk—she had that tense, nervy look on her face—but I shrank back into the corner, pretending to read

27

my book, praying she'd leave me alone. It was great to be away without Dad, but I couldn't face talking about Luke.

'I don't want anything big,' she started, pulling my book down slightly, forcing me to look at her. 'Just a few words to mark the date and the fact that it's been ten years. We could go to the beach, find a nice quiet spot…' She picked up one of the little sugar packets lying in her saucer, tearing off tiny bits of paper until the sugar started to spill out.

'You're not expecting *me* to say anything, are you?'

She glanced down, scared to meet my eye. 'Well, I did think it would be nice if all three of us joined in the ceremony, you know, said a few words or read out a poem. Perhaps you could write your own poem?'

'But, Mum, what would I say? I was only three when Luke died. And why are you calling it a ceremony? It sounds so formal, like it's a funeral or something.'

Mum flinched, shrinking back as if I'd raised my hand to hit her. 'I wish you wouldn't argue with me, Lizzie,' she pleaded. 'Just for once. A few words, that's all I'm asking.'

I looked back down at my book, irritation surging through me. I didn't want to say a few words about Luke. At least, not ones that Mum would want to hear. Like, *Why did you have to go and die? Why did you leave me here with them? Why did you ruin my life?*

It was worse once we were up in the air. Mum was serious about me writing a poem. She gave me a notepad and pen and then sat there watching me, as if I was going to come out with some brilliant masterpiece just like that, right there on the plane. I pushed the notebook back at her and took out my diary, doodling a load of words that rhyme with Luke, like *puke*, *fluke* and *spook*. Mum tried to see what I was writing, but I covered the page with my arm.

I reckoned I could write a pretty good poem but it wouldn't be one Mum would approve of— or let me read out at this stupid ceremony she was planning. I shuddered at the thought. Our holidays to Spain were bad enough without some morbid memorial to mark the anniversary of Luke's death. They could leave me well out of it as far as I was concerned.

As soon as we were through passport control I raced ahead to get my suitcase. Mum was beginning to get that awful, haunted look in her eyes. It happens every year. She seems to cope okay when we're at home, but the second we arrive in Spain it's like she gets caught up in the grief of losing Luke all over again.

I used to enjoy coming here when I was really little, four or five, six even; I looked forward to it for weeks. But that was before I realized what the holidays to Spain were really about. That they weren't holidays at all—just a chance for Mum and Dad to relive what happened to Luke, like watching some sort of awful video clip stuck on a loop, playing over and over again.

Mum had hired a car; a small, bright red Citroën. It took ages to sort out the paperwork and we had a job squeezing all our bags into the tiny boot, but eventually she pulled out of the airport and onto the main road that leads down to the coast. I started to get a heavy feeling, like something pressing down on my chest. Everything was exactly the same; the suffocating heat, the view out of the window, even the smell of the citrus and vanilla air-freshener hanging from the mirror at the front of the car.

'Who was that you were talking to when you rushed off to get your suitcase?' said Mum, glancing over at me.

'No one. Just some girl who had exactly the same case as me. I picked it up by mistake but then mine came round a few seconds later.'

Mum smiled. 'That happened to me once, believe it or not, except I actually took the wrong suitcase home. It was such a muddle, but at least it was at the *end* of the holiday. Imagine how awful it would be if you lost your suitcase at the beginning...'

She was trying to smooth things over. Make friends. She always does that when we row. I stared out of the window, trying to wish myself away. Her voice was so irritating that I wanted to block it out, pretend I was on my own. I'd thought a week away together would be okay—that we might actually have a good time without Dad there to spoil things—but not if she was going to spend most of the time talking about Luke and the ten-year anniversary.

*   *   *

There are two hotels at the Costa de las Cuevas resort. *La Cueva Secreta*, The Secret Cave, and *Bahía de las Cuevas*, Bay of Caves. We always stayed in a sea-view room at The Secret Cave.

It's much bigger and more expensive than the Bay of Caves, with a fancy marble reception area and over a hundred rooms. It's the same hotel we were staying in when Luke died.

A smart-looking woman in a blue uniform greeted us from behind the reception desk.

'Good afternoon, Mrs. Michaels,' she said, smiling. 'I'm Alana. Welcome to *La Cueva Secreta*. I'll call someone to help you with your luggage in just a minute, but please could you first fill out these registration forms.' She handed Mum a form on a clipboard with a pen attached and then turned away to answer the phone.

'Excuse me, please.' A small man in a different coloured uniform slipped out from behind one of the huge marble pillars, shuffling towards us. Mum turned round.

'Mrs. Michaels?'

'Yes.'

'I have important message for you,' he hissed, holding out a folded piece of paper.

'Oh thank you, that's very kind,' said Mum quickly. She grabbed the note out of the man's hand and turned away to read it.

'What's that?' I said, trying to peer over her shoulder. 'Who would leave a message for us *here*?'

Mum shook her head. 'It's nothing,' she muttered, screwing the note up and stuffing it in her pocket. 'It's not even for us.'

'Why are you keeping it then?' I said, looking round to see if the man was still there.

'Please don't start nagging.'

And then I realized, my heart sinking. 'It's not to do with the memorial, is it?'

31

'No, of course not, it's *nothing*.' She turned back to the desk, flustered. It was so obvious she was lying. 'Come on, Lizzie, let me finish filling out these forms and then we can go and get settled in our rooms.'

*   *   *

I got changed as quickly as I could and then went through to Mum's room to ask her if I could go down to the beach. She was still unpacking and seemed nervous about letting me go off by myself, even though we'd been to the resort so many times before.

'No talking to anyone and no wandering off,' she said, sounding just like Dad. It was the same list of rules he always gave me on the first day of the holiday. 'Stay away from the caves,' she went on. 'Don't spend too long in the sun, and absolutely *no* swimming in the sea.'

I rolled my eyes. 'Okay, anything else?'

'I mean it, Lizzie, and make sure you keep your phone switched on so I know where you are when I come down. I shouldn't be too long.'

'Yes, Mum, I will. I always do, don't I?'

I escaped from her room as fast as I could, hurrying down the corridor towards the lifts. It was all such a joke anyway. Who was I going to go off with? Who was I going to talk to? I couldn't even remember the last time I'd had a normal conversation with someone else my age. All I ever did when we came to Spain was sit up on a rock, on the beach, with one of the books Dad forced me to read. He should have saved his stupid rules for someone who actually had a life.

Sometimes I think about what it would be like if Luke hadn't died. I'd probably have gone to a normal school and made normal friends. Dad blamed Luke's death on the friends he made when he started secondary school. He was always telling me what a bad influence they were; how they corrupted his perfect son. It was crazy, but the older I got the more convinced he seemed to be that I was going to turn out exactly the same. That was why he insisted on homeschooling me.

I pressed the button for the lift and a few moments later the silent, silver doors slid open and I stepped inside. It only took a few moments to reach the reception area. I waited for the doors to slide open again, catching a fleeting glimpse of myself in the tinted glass mirror: cropped blonde hair, blue eyes and deathly-white skin.

People say I'm the image of Luke, they say we could've been twins, and they're right up to a point. He had the same blond hair and blue eyes as me, the same pale skin. But judging by the photos that plaster the walls at home, Luke was always smiling—his eyes bright and sparkly— bursting with life. At least when he was alive he was *really* alive. I know it sounds weird, but sometimes, next to Luke, it feels as if I'm the one who died.

Bee

We were staying in a small, family-run hotel just along the coast called the Bay of Caves. Nothing too fancy but perfect for us. It had twelve rooms, a smallish swimming pool, and then steps down to a gorgeous, crescent-shaped bay with the softest sand and turquoise-blue sea. A plump, smiley man called Carlos showed us to our rooms. Mum and Nan were sharing a double with a pretty, white-tiled bathroom and a tiny balcony. Mine was a single with an even tinier balcony, just about big enough for one person.

'What do you think of this then, Val?' said Nan, pressing the big double bed to check it was firm enough. I glanced at Nan. Did she already know that Dad wasn't coming with us when she booked the rooms? Is that why Mum left the tickets out in the kitchen? So Dad would see them and change his mind?

'It's lovely,' Mum admitted, 'but I really hope you're not going to snore.'

She'd hardly said a word since we'd left the airport. She still seemed tense, but I could see she was trying to lighten the mood.

'*Me* snore!' cried Nan. 'The barefaced cheek of it! You're the one who sounds like a dying goose every time you close your eyes. I've never snored in my life.'

'A dying goose? Oh, that's charming,' said Mum, and they were off.

They carried on trading insults, each one worse than the last, as we changed into our swimsuits

34

and headed down to the pool. Nan 'sounded like a foghorn', Mum 'like a cow giving birth'. Nan was 'loud enough to drown out a crowd at a football match', Mum 'a herd of stampeding elephants'. I started to laugh in the end, it was so ridiculous. How on earth were they going to share a room for two weeks?

Carlos was in the reception area helping another couple, but he stopped for a moment and beckoned us over as we came out of the lift.

'This very nice boat trip,' he beamed, holding out some leaflets and vouchers. 'And please come to hotel paella night on Friday. We have music and dancing and very much tasty rice. It's the best.'

'Thank you,' said Nan, taking the leaflets. 'We like a bit of paella, don't we, Val?'

She turned to Mum, but Mum was staring at Carlos with a look of total horror on her face, as if he'd just grown an extra head right in front of her eyes.

'*Val!*' Nan nudged her and then turned back towards Carlos. 'We'd love to come, Carlos, thank you so much.'

'Oh sorry,' said Mum, blinking and shaking her head slightly. 'Yes, we'd love to come. Of course we would.'

'What was that about?' hissed Nan as we walked off in the direction of the pool. 'Why were you staring at the poor man like that?'

'It was just something he said,' muttered Mum.

'What? What did he say? *Boat trip? Paella?*'

'Just drop it, will you?' snapped Mum. She looked back over her shoulder, frowning slightly. 'Listen, I've got to pop back to the room for a second; I've forgotten something. You two go

35

ahead without me.'

It was busy by the pool. Nan nabbed the last two sunbeds and started to smother herself in cream. We actually tan quite easily, all three of us, but we weren't used to this kind of heat. 'Doesn't the water look lovely?' she said. 'I'd jump straight in if I was your age, Bee.' The pool did look tempting but I wanted to be by myself for a bit, to think about everything that had happened. I left her settled on her sunbed with her bumper crossword book and went off to explore.

It was even busier down on the beach, with almost every centimetre of sand covered in brightly coloured towels. There was a small cafe called *Globo Rojo*, with bright red balloons tied to every chair, a hut renting out deckchairs, two lifeguards up in a tall, wooden tower—and a long line of children running in and out of the water, shrieking and dashing back every time a wave came rushing towards them. I picked my way through the towels and down to the water's edge.

I love being by the sea. I just love the feeling of space—the way you can look out across the waves and pretend it goes on for ever. Sometimes, when I'm stuck at school, I like to imagine that I'm far out in the middle of the ocean where no one can get me.

It only took me a few minutes to walk the entire length of the little crescent bay. I sat down for a bit, sifting sand through my fingers, thinking about Dad and how much he would've loved it here too. I tried to picture him over at Uncle Ron's, spending time with my cousins when he should've been here with us. It just felt so wrong coming away without him.

We used to have family holidays when I was a

baby and Aidan was twelve or thirteen. I've seen photos of us on a beach just like this one. I'm sitting in a hole in the sand and Aidan's waving a spade about and Dad's reaching for me, laughing his head off. He looks so young and happy, it's difficult to believe it's the same person.

A couple of children ran past me, chasing a frisbee. I swivelled round to see where it would land and noticed a girl, about my age, perched up on a rock, reading. She was incredibly pale, with short blonde hair tucked under a straw sun hat, and long legs drawn up to her chin. There was something familiar about her—nothing specific, just a feeling I'd maybe seen her somewhere before. I sneaked another look, trying not to make it too obvious, and then I realized: it was the girl from the airport.

I sat watching her for a bit. She was reading one of my favourite books, *Five Children and It*, by E. Nesbit. It was the perfect book to be reading on a beach; about five children and an extremely grumpy sand-fairy who can grant them a single wish each day—but only if he's in a good mood. I don't know anyone else who's read it but it's brilliant.

The other girls in my year tease me about loving books so much. Melissa Knight started it. She got them to call me 'Bookworm Bee' and buzz around behind my back as if they'd just invented the world's funniest joke. I thought they'd get bored after a bit, find someone else to make fun of. I even tried to laugh along with them, but that just seemed to make it worse. If *I* could make a wish, I'd wish for a new friend. Someone brave enough to stand up to Melissa Knight and all her stupid, brainless mates.

The children grabbed their frisbee and raced

off, laughing. The girl on the rock hadn't looked up once from her book, but I was certain she knew I was there. I was dying to talk to her but I didn't want her to think I was stalking her, especially after what happened at the airport. I sat there for at least another five minutes trying to think of something to say that wouldn't sound too desperate, and then forced myself to get up and go over.

'Are you from England?' I said, pressing my toes deep into the warm sand. 'Only we met at the airport...you know, when we were getting our cases.' She didn't say anything. She didn't even blink. 'Erm...I've read that b-book by the way,' I stuttered, wishing I could disappear. 'Do you like it? It's one of my favourites.'

She looked up then, squinting in the sun. Her face was small and pinched, her eyes the exact same colour as the sea.

'Yes, I am from England,' she said, waving the book at me. 'And no, I don't like it—it's rubbish!'

I took a step back, surprised, and neither of us said anything for a moment. The silence seemed to go on for ages. I wracked my brains for something else to say but it was hopeless. I was about to turn away, head back to Mum and Nan at the hotel, when she shifted up suddenly, patting the space beside her and smiling. You'd never believe a smile, even a small one, could change someone's face so completely.

'Look, why don't you come and sit up here,' she said. 'There's loads of room. My name's Lizzie, by the way, what's yours again?'

'I'm Bee,' I said, scrambling up the rock, squashing up next to her. 'Bee Brooks, from England.'

38

And even without a grumpy sand-fairy to grant me my wish, in a funny sort of way, it was as easy as that.

Lizzie

I'd noticed the girl sitting near my rock for ages before she came over; it would have been hard not to, with her wild, curly hair and gorgeous toffee-coloured skin. She was wearing baggy blue shorts with a white vest and she was so brown she looked as if she'd already spent three weeks in the sun.

She asked me if I was from England and if I remembered her from the airport. I did, of course—I even remembered that her name began with a B—but I didn't say anything at first, or even look up. I thought she'd get the hint and go away but she just stood there, peering up at me, shielding her eyes from the sun with her hand.

It seemed so mean to ignore her, but I knew Dad would go mad if he found out I'd been chatting to some stranger on the beach. And then suddenly it hit me. Dad wasn't here; he was hundreds of miles away in England. My tummy flipped over. It was as if I'd been set free from prison. I could speak to whoever I wanted, whenever I wanted, and there was nothing he could do to stop me.

'Yes, I am from England,' I said, holding up the book. 'And no, I don't like it—it's rubbish!'

She stepped back, staring down at her feet.

39

There was this long silence—it seemed to drag on for ever. She looked so nervous, as if she wanted to sink into the sand and disappear. I don't even know why I barked at her like that—it wasn't exactly friendly. The last thing I wanted to do was scare her off.

'Look, why don't you come and sit up here,' I said, smiling. 'There's loads of room. My name's Lizzie, by the way, what's yours again?'

She clambered up, her face breaking into a massive grin, and squashed up next to me on my rock. I felt like cheering. Dad would go ballistic if he ever found out, but I'd worry about that when it happened. I really couldn't see what harm it could do—and anyway, who else did I have to talk to?

'Are you staying at the Bay of Caves?' she asked. 'It's the small hotel just up those steps at the far end of the beach.'

I twisted round, pointing. 'No, I'm staying over there, on the other side of the bay at The Secret Cave. We always stay there, *every* year. Same hotel, same two weeks. It gets so boring you wouldn't believe. How about you? Have you ever been here before?'

Bee shook her head. 'I've never been *anywhere*. This is the first time we've had a proper family holiday since I was tiny and I'm twelve now!'

'Hey, I'm twelve too. What year are you in?'

'Just finished Year Seven, going into Year Eight. How about you?'

'Same,' I said. 'Except I don't go to school, worse luck, I'm homeschooled.'

She stared at me, amazed, as if I'd just said I'd won the lottery or something. 'You are *so* lucky;

I'd do anything to be homeschooled. *Anything*. I hate my school.'

'*Lucky?*' I cried. 'You've got to be joking. I *hate* being homeschooled. It's really grim. I'd swap places with you any day.'

'You wouldn't, believe me, not if you went to my school.' She was quiet for a moment. 'So why are you reading *Five Children and It* if you think it's rubbish?' she asked, changing the subject.

'I have to read it. My dad chose it for me. He chooses all my books. He's given me a list for the holiday and this was the first one—I started it at the airport.'

'What do you mean, he chooses all your books?' She frowned slightly as if she hadn't heard right. 'How does he even know what you'll like?'

I shrugged, embarrassed. 'He doesn't really care what I like. He's the one who homeschools me so he gets to decide.'

My phone buzzed in my pocket suddenly, making us both jump. 'That'll be my mum, checking up on me.'

'Is she really strict?'

'She's not, but my dad is. He's not actually here yet, but my mum still worries about me.'

I texted back that I was on my reading rock and that everything was fine and then stuffed my phone back in my pocket. I wasn't about to mention Bee—Mum would only come scurrying down to make sure she was the right sort of friend for her precious daughter. She's not nearly as bad as Dad but she's too scared to go against any of his stupid rules.

We chatted for ages. Bee seemed really

shy at first but the more we talked, the more she relaxed. She told me how much she loved reading, especially the classics. She said she liked to imagine she was living in the past, in one of those grand, old houses, like Estella in *Great Expectations*. 'The girls at my school tease me about how much I love books and reading...' She hesitated for a moment, biting her lip, as if she was worried I might laugh at her as well, but I told her how much I loved reading too; just not the books my dad chose for me.

'*Little Women* is the only classic I really love,' I told her. 'My dad forced me to read it for this literacy unit we were doing, but I've read it at least three times since then.'

'You're kidding!' cried Bee, her face lighting up. 'I love *Little Women* as well! Jo's my favourite sister; she's just so strong-minded and sure of herself. How about you?'

'I like all of them, to be honest,' I said. 'I think it's because I'm an only child and I've always dreamed of having a big family with lots of sisters!'

My eyes started to sting suddenly. Why did I say that? Why did I say I was an only child? I wanted to unsay it, stuff the words back in my mouth, but it was too late.

'I know exactly what you mean,' said Bee. 'I feel like an only child too, especially since my older brother Aidan left home. He's twelve years older than me so we haven't really got much in common.'

'Do you still see him?' I said. 'Do you text or meet up?'

She shook her head. 'Not really. He doesn't

get on with my dad so he only comes round at Christmas and sometimes on my mum's birthday. We used to get on okay when I was much younger, but he's like a stranger these days.'

I thought about how the 'real' Luke was a stranger to me too and pulled my arms even tighter around my knees. It was weird that we both had older brothers, but that's where the similarity ended. Bee still saw her brother. He was still around. He might have fallen out with her dad and left home but he wasn't dead.

I stared out across the sea, wishing I was somewhere else. I didn't want to talk about Luke, or explain why we came here every year, but telling Bee I was an only child felt wrong, as if I was trying to pretend he'd never existed in the first place.

'What's it like around here?' Bee said after a bit. 'My nan said something about hidden caves.'

I dragged my eyes back to her face. 'Well, there's a boring old cave that all the tourists visit. They call it the "secret" cave but it's not really secret because everyone knows about it. And then there are these other caves just behind the cliffs. *Cueva* actually means "cave" in Spanish. Hey, why don't we go and explore tomorrow? We could meet up straight after breakfast if you like.'

Bee nodded, her eyes shining. 'That would be amazing,' she said. 'I'll have to ask my mum, but I'm sure she'll say it's okay.'

We carried on chatting, swapping stories about our lives back home. It was so nice to be hanging out with someone my own age, talking about normal teenage stuff. I tried to think of a way of explaining about Luke so Bee would understand,

43

but it was impossible to find the right moment. I didn't really get why it was bothering me so much anyway; it wasn't as if telling the truth would change anything.

When it got too hot we slid off the rock and ran down to the sea for a quick paddle. We held our arms out to balance, pressing our toes into the sand as the water surged over our feet and back out again.

'Doesn't it feel lovely?' said Bee. 'I'd love to go in.'

'Me too, but my mum would have a fit. I don't know why she's so worried about it; it's completely safe, especially with the lifeguards watching...' I trailed off, looking over my shoulder at the two lifeguards on duty. They were both drop-dead gorgeous—tall and tanned, with dark glasses and long, sun-streaked hair.

'Hey, Bee, which one do you like best? The one in the red shorts or the one with the mega-muscly arms?'

Bee twisted round to look. 'I don't know,' she giggled. 'Which one do *you* like?'

'Well, the one in the red shorts is taller, but the one with the muscles—'

'Oh my God, they've noticed us!' cried Bee suddenly, grabbing my arm.

'Dare you to wave at them!' I laughed. 'Go on!'

'No way! They might think I need saving or something and how embarrassing would that be?'

'What do you mean, *embarrassing*? It would be brilliant! They might even give you the kiss of life if you're really lucky!' I pretended to swoon, falling back into the sand. 'Quick, call them over! I feel faint! I need some first aid!'

Bee started to laugh. 'Stop it!' she said, grabbing my arm and trying to pull me up. 'They're still watching! Get up, before they come over!'

I jumped up and we skipped out of the water, racing back to my rock. I couldn't believe I'd made a friend so easily—it was amazing. Bee was so nice and easy to talk to. I knew we'd only just met—and that Dad would be furious if he ever found out—but by the time Mum texted me again, asking me to meet up with her, and Bee went back to find her mum and nan, I felt really happy, as if I'd made my first real friend.

Bee

Nan was still sitting by the pool when I got back, with Mum curled up like a cat on the sunbed next to her, fast asleep. As soon as Nan spotted me coming up the steps, she put her finger to her lips to warn me not to wake her.

'She must have exhausted herself with all her worrying,' she whispered, tucking her legs up to make room for me on the end of her sunbed. 'Did you have a nice time? I saw you perched up on a rock, chatting to someone.'

I nodded, smiling. 'I met a really nice girl called Lizzie. She was a bit scary at first but once we started chatting we got on really well. She's staying at the next hotel along, the really posh one, and we've arranged to meet up tomorrow, if that's okay.'

45

'Course it is,' said Nan. 'As long as you're sensible. We'll go up and get changed for dinner in a bit—you must be starving.'

I leaned back against her knees, turning my face up to the sun. 'I love it here, Nan. Seriously, I'm *so*, so pleased we came. If only Dad was here to enjoy it with us, it would be perfect.'

Nan sighed, wrapping her arms round me from behind. 'It's a difficult time, but try not to get too upset. Sometimes you have to leave the grown-ups to do the worrying.'

'I know, but I wish Mum would tell me what's really going on…'

'She will,' said Nan, pulling me closer. 'Just give her some time.'

*   *   *

Mum didn't want to go too far for dinner so we ate at the hotel tapas bar. Carlos showed us to our table, complimenting Nan on how lovely she looked.

'*¡Qué bella!*' he cried, looking her up and down. 'You are like the English rose.'

'You've got an admirer there,' said Mum. 'Perhaps Bee and I should sit at a separate table?'

'Don't be daft, Val,' said Nan, turning scarlet. 'He probably says that to all the ladies. It's just the Spanish way.'

We ordered lots of little dishes from the menu— fried rings of squid, cod cooked with tomatoes and some strange-sounding sausage. I chose *patatas bravas*, chunky chips with spicy mayonnaise. Before the food arrived, Carlos brought over a big jug of sangria: red wine with chunks of fruit floating

46

on top. 'It's for you,' he said, winking at Nan. 'No charge for my pretty *señorita*.'

'He's totally smitten,' said Mum, trying not to laugh. '*My pretty* señorita*!*'

I glanced across the table at Nan. She looked about five years younger and we'd only been here for a day. She probably needed the holiday more than any of us. She always tries to look on the bright side and stay positive, but it took her ages to smile again after my granddad Harry died last year. She's the sort of person who puts a brave face on even when she feels like crying.

It didn't take long for the food to arrive. Nan said the squid was the best she'd ever tasted, but I pushed the dish away when she offered it to me.

'I'll stick to the potatoes, thanks,' I said, shuddering. 'I don't know how you can eat sliced up baby octopus. It's gross.'

'There's no need for that, Bee,' said Mum. She still seemed a bit tense, snapping at me for no reason, although she did nudge me every time Carlos found a reason to come over to our table. I wondered if she was missing Dad as much as I was, but I didn't dare ask in case it put her in a bad mood again.

About halfway through the meal some Spanish dancers appeared, dressed in these amazing costumes and waving fans. They weaved in and out of the tables, snapping brightly painted castanets above their heads as they went. Nan started to sway from side to side, clicking her fingers and singing along.

'Oh, aren't they good,' she cried above the music. 'I really feel like I'm on holiday now.'

Bailey texted me towards the end of the meal

47

to say it was still raining at the campsite. I texted him back that it was boiling hot in Spain and that we were having a great time. I took a photo of Nan and Carlos singing along to the music and attached it to the message, with the caption, *True Love!*

Just before we went upstairs at the end of the meal, Carlos came over with another leaflet.

'We have boat trip tomorrow, *cueva secreta,* is to secret cave,' he explained. 'I very much like you to come.'

'That's very nice of you, thank you,' said Nan, beaming at Carlos as she took the leaflet. 'Night-night now.'

Carlos gave a little bow and backed away.

'Free wine, secret caves, whatever next?' laughed Mum.

Nan started to blush again. 'Behave yourself! He's just being friendly. This sounds good though,' she said, reading the leaflet. 'A two-hour trip around the bay, and then through a secret cave to the other side of the resort. You could ask your new friend to come if you'd like, Bee.'

'What friend?' said Mum, her face full of concern suddenly. 'You didn't say anything about a friend. I don't want you going off with someone we don't know.'

'It's *fine*, Mum. She's staying at the next hotel and she's really nice, and we're not going off *anywhere*.'

'Well, I suppose that's okay, but...'

'Don't worry, Val,' said Nan. 'We can meet her tomorrow, can't we, Bee?'

I nodded, grateful to Nan. 'She's really nice,' I said. 'You'll like her.'

It was far too hot to sleep that night. I could hear Mum and Nan arguing through the bedroom wall, something to do with Dad again. I crept out of bed and pressed my ear against the wall, but it was difficult to make out exactly what they were saying. It was obvious Mum was really upset though.

I got back into bed and lay there as they droned on, thinking about Lizzie, and how pleased I was that I'd found the courage to go over and talk to her. I'd never have had the guts to do that at school. The girls in my year were all so busy trying to impress Melissa Knight they wouldn't dare make friends with someone like me.

Lizzie

Mum ordered room service for supper. It seemed like a weird thing to do on the first night of our holiday, especially as it was such a warm evening, but she said the journey had worn her out. As soon as she'd finished her meal she lay back on the huge double bed and closed her eyes.

'I'm sorry, Lizzie,' she said, yawning. 'I'm just exhausted.'

I sat on the end of the bed, watching her. She looked so small, more like a child than an adult. I twisted the end of the sheet round my finger. What was I supposed to do all evening if she went to sleep? I was beginning to feel just as trapped here as I did at home. I bet Bee was

49

having a better time with her mum and nan. 'Do you even enjoy coming here?' I said after a bit. 'Not just to Spain, but to the same hotel, year after year?'

Mum didn't move for a moment and I wondered if she was already asleep, but then she pulled herself up, leaning back against the velvet headboard.

'I don't enjoy it,' she said slowly, as if she was trying to find the right words. 'It's just something I feel I have to do.'

'But it's so morbid. The same hotel, the same two weeks.'

She gave me a small smile. 'I know it seems morbid to you, and I know it's not really fair dragging you back here every year. It's just that when I'm in England, life carries on and we're all so busy and sometimes it almost feels normal and that's scary...' She took a deep breath. 'So you see I have to come here. I have to come so I can slow down and remember my Luke...' She trailed off, blinking fast.

'And what about Dad?'

'What about him?'

'Does he enjoy coming back here every year? Raking over the past. Or does he just come because of you?'

'It's complicated with your dad, Lizzie. He doesn't like to talk about it, but he's still so angry about what happened the night Luke died.'

I stared at her. 'But it was an accident, wasn't it? You've always said Luke died in an accident, so who's he angry with?'

She shrugged, biting her lip. 'He's just angry,' she said. 'At me, at himself, at the world...'

'And me,' I said.

She shook her head hard. 'No, not at you, Lizzie. He's not angry with you. He's just so full of anger, there's no room left for anything else.'

Bee

Breakfast was served on a small terrace at the back of the hotel. Mum was still in bed when I went down. Nan said she'd had a bad night, too much rich food, but I was pretty sure it was more to do with their row and Dad not being here than with the food. I gulped down a glass of freshly squeezed orange juice, grabbed a slice of toast and raced down to the beach. I couldn't wait to see Lizzie and tell her about the boat trip.

She was waiting for me up on the rock, wearing her floppy hat, her knees drawn up to her chin, exactly like the day before. I was so relieved to see her. I called out and she looked up, waving.

'Hey, there's a trip to the secret cave,' I said, scrambling up the rock to sit with her. 'The boat leaves at twelve and it lasts for two hours. I know you said everyone goes there, but it sounds really good. They give you lunch and everything.'

Lizzie pulled a face. 'Yeah, I know about that trip, but my mum won't let me go. You don't know what it's like, Bee. I might as well be locked up in prison. I'm not allowed to do anything.'

'But she lets you come down here.'

'I know, but only because my dad's not around. She'll still be checking up on me all the time. Look...' She pulled her phone out her pocket.

51

'She's already texted me twice and I've only been sitting here for twenty minutes.'

'It doesn't matter,' I said quickly, sorry I'd mentioned it. 'We can explore by ourselves. My mum wasn't too keen either, to be honest.'

We sat in the early morning sunshine, watching the beach fill up. It was brilliant being up on the rock, looking down at everyone, as if we were in charge of the whole resort. It made me realize even more just how lonely I'd been at Glendale. We laughed about the mix-up with our cases and Lizzie rolled her eyes when I told her how confident she'd looked at the airport, as if she spent her whole life travelling the world.

'Travelling to *Spain*, you mean,' she said. 'This is the only place we ever come.'

'Your parents must really like it then, if they come back every year.'

She shrugged, staring out to sea. 'Not really. How about your parents? How come your dad's not here with you?'

'He doesn't like holidays,' I said, my face growing hot. I nibbled at the skin around my thumbnail. I wasn't sure how much to tell her. I didn't want to blurt out all my troubles when I'd only known her for a day. Dad disappearing for three days and the police coming round wasn't exactly the easiest thing to explain. I wondered if he'd answered any of my texts yet, but I'd left my phone back at the hotel so I couldn't check.

'If I could choose any holiday in the world,' Lizzie was saying, 'I'd go to America or Africa or India—I'd never come to Spain again for the rest of my life! How about you? Where would you go?'

'Oh, I'm not sure. I've never really *been*

anywhere. But I love the ocean. I know it sounds silly, but I just love how big it is—the way it seems to go on for ever and ever.'

'It doesn't sound silly at all,' said Lizzie. 'I know exactly what you mean. You could never feel trapped if you were out at sea.'

I nodded, agreeing.

'But even better than that,' she said, her eyes gleaming, 'you could get the person you hate the most in the world, stick them in a boat and push them out to sea and you'd never have to set eyes on them ever again. Wouldn't that be brilliant?'

'Brilliant!' I said, imagining Melissa Knight adrift in the middle of the ocean. 'Who would you put in?'

'My dad, obviously,' she said without hesitating. 'And I wouldn't miss him one tiny bit! How about you?'

'Oh, just some girl at my school,' I said, shivering in the heat. How could she have that effect on me when she was so far away? Sometimes it felt as if she'd got right inside me—as if I'd never get rid of her, however far away I was.

'Oh no, look at my arms!' cried Lizzie suddenly, holding them out to me. 'I'll burn to a crisp if we sit on this rock any longer. Honestly, you don't know how lucky you are that you tan so easily.'

We helped each other down and made our way over to the little cafe, grabbing a table with a big sunshade, and ordering two glasses of ice-cold lemonade.

'*Globo Rojo* means Red Balloon by the way,' said Lizzie, sipping her drink. 'One of the waiters who worked here told me last year. That's why they tie red balloons to the chairs.'

'Do you know lots of people at the resort then?'

She shook her head. 'Not really. He was just chatting to me one day when I was sitting here with my mum and dad. I was dreading this holiday to be honest. It was so boring last year, and the year before...'

'What did you do?'

'Nothing much really. Hung out at the beach, pretended to read, tried to get a tan.'

'Well, it doesn't have to be like that this year,' I said shyly. 'We could meet up every day if you like.'

'We could, but not *every* day,' she said, her voice hard suddenly. 'There's one day when I've got to do something with my parents.' She stared off over my shoulder, her face closing up for a moment. I was about to ask her what was wrong when she looked back at me, blinking. 'Hey, why don't we go and explore the other caves I told you about yesterday? It's so unbearably hot, even under this umbrella.'

'Okay.' I nodded. 'I'll just go and tell my mum. Wait for me here.'

The caves were on the other side of the bay, more or less hidden from view. I left Lizzie at the cafe and ran back to the pool. Mum was perched on the end of her sunbed, talking to someone on the phone, but she got up and walked away the second she saw me coming. It had to be Dad—why else would she do that? My stomach clenched up, half in fear, half in excitement.

'Oh, hello, Bee,' said Nan. 'Where's your friend?'

'She's not allowed on the boat trip to the secret cave, so we thought we'd go and explore the caves down on the beach. Is that okay?'

'Yes, it's fine, but don't you want something to

eat first?'

'No thanks, I'm too hot. Is Mum okay? Is she talking to Dad?'

Nan glanced over at Mum. Her shoulders were hunched over and she was clutching a tissue. 'Don't worry about your mum, she's fine, honestly. Just look after yourself, won't you, and try to stay out of the sun for a bit.'

I nodded, my eyes still fixed on Mum. It was so frustrating the way neither of them would tell me anything. I was tempted to hang about until she came off the phone, but Lizzie was waiting for me. I'd just have to make sure to speak to her later. I leaned down to give Nan a kiss.

And that's when I saw it.

An envelope sticking out of Mum's beach bag.

A *pale pink* envelope, just like the one that had arrived a few weeks ago, but with no stamp or address, just Mum's name handwritten on the front.

I sank down on the deckchair next to Nan, my mouth suddenly so dry I could hardly speak.

'What's that?' I croaked.

'What's what, love?'

'That letter. In Mum's bag.' I glanced up at Mum. She was still on the phone with her back to us.

'Oh, that,' said Nan slowly. She was wearing her sunglasses, so it was impossible to know if she was surprised or what her reaction was at all. 'That's from an old friend of your mum. Carlos delivered it this morning while we were having breakfast, but you'd already gone down to the beach.'

'But it's just like the other letter. That was in a pink envelope, just like this one.'

55

'You've lost me, love,' said Nan, pushing her sunglasses onto the top of her head. 'What other letter?'

'Oh come on, Nan! The letter that arrived before Dad went missing. The letter that caused all the rows.'

Nan looked at me for a long time without saying anything.

'So was that letter from Mum's friend too?' I persisted, watching her face. 'I mean, it's the same sort of envelope, so it must have been. I really wish you'd tell me what's going on. Why is this old friend sending Mum letters? Why doesn't she just phone or text?'

'I don't suppose she has the number any more. They lost touch such a long time ago, sweetheart. What about your friend? Isn't she waiting for you down at the beach?'

She was trying to get rid of me. She didn't want me to ask any more questions. Someone was writing to my mum and it was obvious they were linked to what was going on between Mum and Dad. But how would they know Mum was in Spain? And where we were staying? It didn't make any sense. I wiped my palms on my knees. Something weird was going on.

'I really miss my dad,' I said, feeling so far away from him suddenly. 'I don't understand why he hasn't called me, or answered any of my messages. I know it's only been a week since I last saw him, but it feels more like years.'

Nan pulled me to her and hugged me tight. 'Some things are difficult to understand when you're a child, Bee. Your mum and dad are going through a difficult time right now but they're

56

working very hard to sort things out. The best thing you can do for your mum is to have a brilliant time while we're here. She'd really hate it if you let their problems spoil your holiday.'

I hugged her back but I felt more worried than ever. How was I supposed to have a brilliant time when I knew they were going through a 'difficult time'. I trailed back down to the cafe, dragging my feet through the sand, trying to work out if there was any way I could talk to Dad myself. I really wanted to tell him how much I missed him and how confused I was about everything.

Lizzie jumped up as she saw me coming. 'Sorry I was so long,' I said. 'I was with my nan.'

'What's the matter? Did she want you to go on the tourist boat with them?'

I shook my head. 'No, it was nothing like that— there's just something really strange going on.'

'What do you mean?'

'I'm not sure, to be honest.' We started walking towards the caves. 'My mum's acting weird, and my nan won't tell me why, and I really need to talk to my dad.'

'What do you mean, acting weird?'

I shook my head again, shrugging. 'She's usually so together, but she keeps snapping at me and she's on the phone to someone right now in floods of tears. It's something to do with these letters, and the fact that my dad's gone to stay with my uncle, but she won't tell me anything and I've got a horrible feeling they're going to split up.'

Lizzie stopped walking and turned to face me. 'So why don't you just call your dad?' she said. 'You can dial this special code for international calls and you don't even have to pay.'

57

She was right. I should just call Dad. It was exactly what I'd just been thinking myself. But I was scared. Mum said she didn't want me to bother Dad at Uncle Ron's and he hadn't answered any of the messages I'd left on his mobile. I didn't have Uncle Ron's home number either—I'd have to get it off Mum or Nan, and who was to say they'd even give it to me? And what if I spoke to Dad and he said something terrible, like he wasn't coming back home?

'I will call him,' I said to Lizzie, trying to shake off the awful feeling that things were never going to be right again. 'I'll call him at my Uncle Ron's—but in a few days.'

'Come on then,' she said, linking her arm through mine, and we carried on round the bay.

Lizzie

The caves were cut into the back of the jagged cliffs, dark and gaping like a row of hungry mouths waiting to be fed. I'd never actually been inside them before—it was against Dad's rules—but I wasn't going to let that stop me today. There was a rumour that one of the caves was haunted, that a spirit had been trapped in there for hundreds of years, but I wasn't going to let that stop me either!

I led the way, clambering over a mound of rubble and rocks, stumbling along as fast as I could. Bee held back, a bit unsure. 'Come on,' I said, turning round to grab her hand. 'We haven't got much time; my mum will be down to find me

58

soon. She's dragging me off to see some ancient ruins or something.' I pulled her over the rocks and into the first cave we came to. It was cold and damp and reeked of seaweed.

'Are you sure it's safe?' she said, a note of panic in her voice. 'I read this story once about these two children who got trapped inside some caves and no one knew they were there and they had no food or drink and no way to contact anyone and—'

'Calm down, Bee, it's completely safe,' I said, doing my best to reassure her. 'Just follow me. The caves go back really far, deep into the cliffs, but we'll just walk in a straight line and then retrace our steps to get out.'

I kept hold of her arm, leading the way through the darkness. Bee stumbled after me, trying not to freak out too much, but I could tell she was really scared. The cave narrowed suddenly, the walls shrinking in around us. It was so tight we had to walk one in front of the other, without touching. We went a little further and then something brushed past us in the dark.

'What the hell was that?' cried Bee. She shook her head, running her hands through her hair. 'There's something flying around in here!'

I turned to face her, trying not to freak out myself. I didn't want to back out now we'd got this far. 'It's okay, calm down,' I said. 'It was only one of those flying beetles.'

'It wasn't! It was a bat! I swear it was a bat!' She was so close to me, I could feel her breath on my face. 'I really don't like it. I'm sorry, Lizzie, but can we go back now, *please*?'

'Just a tiny bit further, Bee. I'll look after you,

I promise. You don't know how long I've been waiting to explore these caves.'

We squeezed ourselves through the cramped passage for a few more steps and then the ground dropped down slightly, taking us into a big circular space. It was impossible to see anything except the vague outline of the walls. It was like a secret room. I wrapped my arms around myself, shivering. This was easily the most exciting thing I'd done in ages.

'These caves have been here for hundreds and hundreds of years,' I whispered. 'Apparently there used to be treasure hidden in them, left by the Romans, and it was guarded by these vicious dogs who watched over it night and day.'

Bee pressed herself right into me, her voice quivering in the gloom. 'I really don't like it. I know I'm being a wimp, but it's so dark.'

'We'll just stay for a few minutes. There are no vicious dogs these days, I swear.'

I decided to keep quiet about the trapped spirit. I didn't want to freak her out even more. There's no such thing as spirits anyway. When you're dead, you're dead. I don't believe in spooky white ghosts floating through walls, or that Luke is still *with us* in some way, like Mum does. She's been to see all sorts of clairvoyants and mediums to see if she can make contact with him—as if he's up there somewhere, just waiting to have a chat.

'We did a topic on the R-r-romans once,' said Bee suddenly, her voice still shaking. 'It was brilliant. We had a proper Roman banquet, and we made these beautiful mosaics using tiny pieces of broken glass.'

'But I thought you said you didn't like school?'

'This was when I was in *primary* school. I go to Glendale High now and I hate it.'

'Hey, I know Glendale High. It's that really posh girls' school with the purple uniform. It's right near where I live!'

'I don't believe you!' cried Bee. 'You live near *Glendale High*?'

'Just a few streets away. The girls who go there are all rich and stuck up, aren't they?'

Bee snorted. 'Well, don't start thinking I'm like that. I only go there because I won a scholarship—and most days I wish I'd never even sat the exam in the first place.'

'I still think you're lucky. I never get to do anything fun like banquets or mosaics. It's just literacy, French, maths and science at my house.'

'Oh, I love literacy,' said Bee, her voice a little stronger. 'Not just reading. I really love writing as well. I've got a big literacy topic to do this summer. We have to pick a theme, anything we like, and write a series of poems.'

'Oh my God, I'm rubbish at writing poems. Have you decided on a theme yet?'

She shook her head in the gloom. 'Not yet, but I've got a few ideas.'

'You could write about Spain, or maybe about ancient caves?'

'Yeah, but you know what it's like with poetry,' said Bee. 'You can't just write about anything, you have to feel really inspired.'

I thought about asking her to help me with the poem for Luke's memorial if she enjoyed poetry so much, but then I'd have to admit that I'd lied to her yesterday about being an only child. Mum was still going on about the poem. She wanted

61

me to come up with some emotional tribute to this amazing brother I was supposed to miss so much. But every time I thought about Luke, especially about Luke dying, I felt like smashing something up—and how was I meant to express that in a poem?

I ran my hands over the solid stone walls. They felt cold and slimy. There were some grooves scratched into the rock; lines or something, carved deep into the stone.

'Hey, look at this.'

Bee turned towards the wall and I lifted her hand up, guiding her fingers over the carved area. 'Can you feel it?'

'Yes, I think it might be letters,' she said. 'Do you think someone's scratched a message?'

I ran my fingers from the top of the first carved-out line and followed it down. 'It is a letter, you're right.'

'What do you think it says?'

'Hang on, I'm not sure.' I started again, straining to see in the dark, pressing my fingers into the rock. 'There are three letters and some dots.' I ran my finger down and round, again and again, but it was impossible to tell what they were supposed to be.

'I can't make it out. You try.'

Bee slipped her hand under mine, tracing the lines and dots again. 'We should've brought a torch,' she said. 'What about your phone? Does the screen light up?'

I took it out of my pocket but it was dead.

'It's not working,' I said, staring down at the blank screen—and feeling the first flicker of fear myself. 'Come on, maybe we should go. I don't want my mum to find out I've been breaking one of my dad's stupid rules.'

'Hang on a sec. Oh my god!'

Bee pulled her hand away, stumbling back.

'What? What's the message? What does it say?'

'R.I.P.,' she said, her voice shaky. 'That's what the letters spell, R.I.P.'

She stumbled back further and I reached out to stop her falling. 'You don't think someone's buried here, do you?' I hissed.

'I don't know,' she said, turning back the way we'd come. 'But I'm not hanging around to find out!' She lurched across the circular space, squeezing herself into the narrow passage.

'Wait a sec,' I said, stuffing my phone back in my pocket. 'It's just a carving on the wall. It doesn't really mean anything.'

I squeezed myself into the passage after her, grabbing hold of the back of her T-shirt as we made our way out. The passage seemed narrower somehow, and much longer. I must've been so excited on the way in that I hadn't noticed how far we'd come. I was just beginning to wonder if we'd ever see light again when the exit came into view. Bee sped up as much as she could and we both stumbled out of the cave.

She stared at me for a minute, blinking in the sun, and then burst out laughing.

'What's so funny?' I said, but then I started to laugh too and once I'd started I couldn't stop. We hung on to each other in hysterics.

'Oh God, I'm so happy we're out!' gasped Bee. 'I swear I thought we were going to die in there. That was *so* creepy.'

I sank down to the ground, wiping my eyes. 'I didn't tell you before, but one of the caves is actually supposed to be haunted.'

Bee stopped laughing and stared at me. 'You are joking.'

'Well, I thought it was only a rumour, but now I'm not so sure.'

She sank down next to me. 'What is the rumour exactly?'

'That someone died in the caves. I don't know how, but apparently their spirit became trapped and it's been knocking about in there for hundreds and hundreds of years.'

Bee's eyes were as big as saucers. 'So what are you saying? That there's a body? Or a grave, or what?'

'I don't know, but I'd love to find out!'

'You're crazy,' she said. 'I'm sorry, Lizzie, but I'm not going searching for dead people or bones or anything like that.'

'Come on, don't be such a killjoy! Think how exciting it would be if we discovered something. We could come back tomorrow and—'

My phone suddenly buzzed in my pocket. I pulled it out.

Three voicemail messages from Mum.

'I'd better get back to the beach,' I said, jumping up. 'I thought my mum might relax a bit without my dad here breathing down our necks, but she seems to be even more uptight than ever.'

Bee

Lizzie and I met up every day after that but we didn't go back to the caves. She was dying to find out more about the message carved into the wall— she had all these gory theories—but I was way too frightened. It wasn't just the fact that it said *R.I.P.*; it was the narrow passage and the smell and the damp, murky gloom. Just the thought of it made my chest tighten up until it was difficult to breathe properly.

I was worried at first that Lizzie might want to go off and explore without me, or that she'd think I was too boring. She had this sort of restless energy, as if she was constantly waiting for something to happen, but the more time we spent together the closer we became—and the closer we became, the more we discovered how similar we were.

Like the fact that we were both born in October: me first and then Lizzie two weeks later. And the fact that we lived in the same part of London, only fifteen minutes away from each other. And then there was the way we both hated school so much— even though she was homeschooled and I was stuck at Glendale High. It was spooky, but it began to feel as if we'd been destined to meet.

'Maybe we were separated at birth,' Lizzie said one morning. 'Torn away from each other and forced to live apart until fate brought us back together.'

I wanted to believe that was true—that we really were sisters—but you only had to look at us to know we weren't related. Lizzie was so pale

65

you could see the faint blue of her veins running under her skin, whereas my tan was getting deeper and deeper by the day. She did this thing every morning where she'd hold her arm out next to mine, groaning at how white she was, desperate to change colour. I don't think she had the first idea about how pretty she was.

She told me about this boy she liked in her road called Dilan. They'd been homeschooled together years ago when they were little, but then he started going to proper school.

'I call him *C.C.* in my diary, just in case my dad ever reads it. It's a kind of code. It stands for Cromwell Corner, because Dilan lives in the corner house at the end of my street.'

'I didn't know you kept a diary. Do you write in it every day?'

'Nearly, apart from when I'm too tired. And I haven't written in it much this holiday. I've been having too much fun! How about you? Do you keep one?'

'I used to when I was younger, but not any more. So do you think Dilan knows you like him?'

'No way. I watch him from my window all the time—he's always in the garden messing about with his bike—and I've even walked past a couple of times, when I've managed to get out of the house. But he never even says hi. I could probably drop dead right in front of him and he still wouldn't notice me.'

'I bet he would,' I said. 'He's probably madly in love with you already; he just doesn't know what to do about it.'

'Don't be stupid!' she cried, turning scarlet. 'And anyway, my dad would rather die than let me have

66

a boyfriend. What about you? Do you like anyone?'

'No…yes…oh, I don't know.' I could feel my face growing as hot as Lizzie's. 'I'm really good friends with my next-door neighbour, Bailey, and I suppose he is cute in a weird sort of way—not like the lifeguards or anything—but we've grown up together like brother and sister.'

'Are you sure about that?' Lizzie teased, as I put my hands up to my flaming cheeks. 'It sounds as if you like him to me.'

'No I don't!'

'Well, I'll just have to check him out when we get back from holiday, won't I?'

I smiled at the thought of Lizzie coming over. It was amazing that she lived so close by. I still didn't get why Nan had booked the holiday in the first place, or what was going on between Mum and Dad, but coming to Spain and meeting Lizzie was easily the best thing that had ever happened to me.

*   *   *

Mum seemed happy enough that I'd made a friend so quickly, although she was so caught up with her own worries that I don't think she noticed what I was doing most of the time. She spent a large part of each day on her own, walking around the resort or sitting in the hotel lounge, reading. I kept meaning to ask her about the letters—I even thought about searching her room when she was down at breakfast or off on one of her walks—but I was too scared. It was easier in a way to hang out with Lizzie and try to pretend that everything was okay.

Some days when it got too hot on the rock,

Lizzie and I would go for a swim in the hotel pool. Nan was always there, relaxing on one of the sunbeds with her bumper book of crosswords and a tall, icy drink. I felt a bit sorry for her, lying there by herself without Mum, but she said it was the first proper break she'd had in years and that she'd never felt better. It was weird how the three of us had come away together, but were all busy doing our own thing.

We'd been at the resort for exactly a week when Lizzie's dad arrived. She'd been dreading it for days, convinced he wouldn't let her out of his sight once he was there. His plane was due to land at four in the afternoon, so we'd arranged to meet up straight after breakfast, worried it might be for the last time.

'I'm not actually going to tell him about you,' she said, as I clambered up the side of the rock to sit with her. 'If we see each other again, it'll have to be in secret.'

'*Really?* What about your mum? Does she know about me?'

'She knows I've made friends with someone, she's seen us together a few times, but I haven't gone into any details. She'd only end up telling my dad and then he'd insist on meeting your mum and nan—and then he'd want to know where we were and what we were doing. It would be a total nightmare.'

'Are you sure he'd be that strict?'

She pulled a face. 'You've got no idea. Look, I know my mum's been texting me non-stop, but it's been brilliant this week, just coming down here every day, hanging out like a normal person—having a laugh with Mum in the evenings. It

68

wouldn't be like that with my dad.'

'I can't believe he's that overprotective. Why is he like that? Why doesn't he let you go to normal school and choose your own friends?'

Lizzie was quiet for a moment. 'I'd do anything to go to a normal school,' she said, not really answering my question. 'It's awful having lessons at home. I have to sit there with him every day and it's SO boring. Just me and my dad, hour after hour. I feel like running away sometimes.'

'That's how I feel about my school,' I said. 'I wish I never had to go back.'

'You keep saying that, Bee, but what's so bad about it?'

I wrapped my arms round my knees, a familiar heavy feeling pressing down on my chest. 'There's just this girl, Melissa Knight. She's been on my case ever since I started last September. She found out I was there on a scholarship and she's been out to get me ever since.'

I'd never told anyone about Melissa, not even Bailey, but I found myself telling Lizzie everything. There was just something about her; the way she sat there taking in every word, her eyes never leaving my face for a moment, as if she understood exactly how I felt. What it felt like to be bullied.

'Why don't you tell your mum and dad, or your nan?' she said when I'd finished. 'Tell them you want to change schools? There must be another school you could go to.'

'I can't. They'd be so disappointed if I said I wanted to leave, especially my dad.'

'Seriously, Bee, I think you should tell them. Do they know *anything*?'

I shook my head. 'I can't tell my mum. She'd

only want to come up to school and get it sorted out and that would just make it a million times worse. She's always going on about how there's a solution to every problem, but there isn't, not to this one. And my dad would just be gutted—he was so proud of me when I won the scholarship.'

'But however proud he was, he wouldn't want you to be unhappy, would he?'

I shrugged, staring out to sea, thinking about Dad. I still hadn't plucked up the courage to ask Mum or Nan for Uncle Ron's number, and Dad still hadn't answered any of the messages I'd left on his mobile. He'd sent me another text, but it had only said hi, and that he hoped I was having a good time. It was weird how much Lizzie was dreading her dad coming, while I was desperate to see mine again.

'What's so special about this Melissa Knight anyway?' said Lizzie suddenly, her turquoise eyes flashing. 'If I ever got to meet her, I'd tell her to take a flying jump!'

'You think you would, but trust me, she's evil. If you knew all the things I'd planned to say to her over the past year, the brilliant put-downs I've practised in my room, but she only has to look at me and I shrivel up like a piece of old leather.'

When I was in Year Six this policewoman came to talk to our class about starting secondary school—about gangs on buses, and older kids offering us drugs. She spelled out all the dangers we might face, but she didn't say anything about nice girls from posh families. Nice girls like Melissa Knight. She was the only danger I'd had to face so far.

'But you wouldn't be scared if I was there, would

you?' said Lizzie. 'I wish I could come and meet you from school one day, when you go back in September. I'd sort her out for you; seriously, I'm not scared of anyone.'

I hugged myself, imagining the scene. Me and Lizzie against Melissa Knight and all her stupid mates. I knew it would never happen, but just the thought of it made me feel better.

*   *   *

We didn't talk about her dad arriving again but Lizzie's mood seemed to sink further and further as the day went on. We had a swim in the pool and then sat at the cafe to share a ham baguette, but she was really quiet, lost in her own thoughts. I'd never seen her so down. She didn't even react when one of the lifeguards came over to buy a bottle of water, smiling at her and flicking one of the red balloons in her direction as he passed our table.

'You're not scared of your dad are you, Lizzie?' I said in the end. 'Only you seem so—'

Her head snapped up. 'Of course I'm not scared!' she interrupted, her eyes cold and hard. 'I told you. I'm not scared of anyone! You're the one who's scared of everything!'

I blinked back tears, shocked at how angry she sounded. She'd never spoken to me like that before. 'I'm sorry, I didn't mean to upset you. I was just trying to understand why you were so...' I trailed off and neither of us said anything for a moment.

'No, *I'm* sorry,' she said after a bit. She looked as if she was going to cry herself. 'I didn't mean it, Bee, I promise; you just don't know what he's like.'

I smiled to show her I wasn't angry. I just wanted to do something to help. Her mum's text came just after three—the phone vibrated on the table between us. She picked it up, staring at the screen, and then stood up, saying she had to go.

'What's going to happen tomorrow?' I said, scared I wouldn't see her again.

She shrugged, pushing the rest of the baguette towards me. 'I'll text you in the morning after breakfast. I'm sure I'll be able to get away at some point. But don't forget, Bee…' She looked around as if she was frightened someone might be listening. 'From now on, everything about our friendship has got to be dead secret.'

Lizzie

Mum was waiting for me just inside the entrance to the hotel. 'I've got a surprise for you,' she said, waving a leaflet at me as I came through the revolving doors. 'Something nice for us to do before Dad gets here.'

'What is it?' I said. The last thing I felt like was a surprise.

'It's a treatment at the hotel beauty spa. I've booked us an hour each. I think I might have my nails done or a facial…' She handed the leaflet to me as we walked towards the lift. 'What do you fancy? Nails? Hair? Anything you like.'

'I don't know,' I said, glancing down at the leaflet. 'I'm not really in the mood, to be honest.'

Mum's face fell. 'Oh come on, Lizzie. A girlie pamper session will be lovely.'

72

'I know, but Dad's coming and—'

'That's exactly why we need to go and do this now,' she said firmly, herding me into the lift. 'I know it's not your sort of thing, but you'll enjoy it once we're there.'

The hotel beauty spa was on the lower-ground floor. There were candles and music and women milling about in white towelling robes. They were all talking in these hushed voices as if they were in a library, and I couldn't see a single person under the age of forty.

'Are you sure I'm not too young?' I whispered, feeling a bit out of place.

Mum shook her head, smiling. 'You're never too young for a bit of pampering. Have you decided what treatment you'd like?'

I ended up having my nails done with Mum. We sat next to each other in our white robes with our hands in hot, perfumed water, trying to decide which colour polish we should choose. It was weird, but I actually began to enjoy myself. There was something very relaxing about the whole thing with the candles and the music and the dimmed lighting. Almost as if we were cocooned from the rest of the world.

The beauty therapist was very friendly, showering me with compliments. She said I had wonderful skin tone and that my eyes were such an unusual colour and that I was so lucky to be a natural blonde.

Mum nodded, agreeing. 'Yes, she's beautiful, isn't she?'

I glanced across at her, embarrassed at all the attention. She was smiling but she had that funny faraway look in her eyes that she gets sometimes, as if she's staring into the past. I was certain suddenly that she was going to say something about Luke—about how similar we were. I held my breath, waiting for her to ruin everything, but she just shook her head slightly, and the moment passed.

It was easily the most relaxed I'd seen her for ages. She told me about this time she'd tried to bleach her hair blonde with a friend, and it had ended up bright green. She said my granddad had gone mad and threatened to cut it all off—but that even though he'd waved the scissors around and shouted a lot, she knew he'd never actually do it.

I think she was trying to make me feel better about Dad arriving—or maybe she was trying to make me feel better about Dad full stop—but it wasn't the same. *Her* dad, my granddad, was strict about normal things like make-up and boyfriends. He was old-fashioned and stuffy, always going on about manners and respect, but he never kept Mum trapped in her own house like a prisoner.

*   *   *

Dad got a taxi from the airport and was due to arrive just after six. Mum and I waited for him downstairs in the lobby area of the hotel. I think Mum was dreading it as much as me—she was a bag of nerves, checking her phone every two minutes to see if he was on his way. She'd probably enjoyed the week away from him as much as I had, even though we hadn't really done that much.

He pushed his way through the revolving door bang on time and strode across the reception area as if he owned the entire hotel. I shrank back in my chair as he came towards us. It had only been a week since I'd last seen him, but he looked bigger than I remembered and more powerful. Mum jumped up to greet him and they talked quietly for a few moments.

I was tempted to sneak away. To run out of the hotel and keep on running until I was as far away from him as I could possibly get. I'd had such a great time hanging out with Bee—it was the most fun I'd had in years—but now Dad was here and the rules would start, with the constant questions about where I was going and who I was seeing, and it would all be ruined.

We went for dinner at a restaurant recommended by the hotel. It was very smart, with air conditioning and waiters in suits, completely different from the beachside cafes Mum and I had been eating at during the first week. I ordered some familiar-sounding fish dish, but when it arrived, the fish still had its head on, with its mouth gaping open and one glassy eye staring up at me.

I didn't know what to do—there was no way I could eat it. I tried some peppers and tomatoes at the side of the dish, but I couldn't bring myself to touch the actual fish. Every time I glanced down at my plate, the pale, glassy eye seemed to be fixed on my face, accusing me, as if I was guilty of killing it myself.

'Come on, Lizzie,' said Dad, waving his fork at me. 'Eat up.'

'I'm not really hungry,' I said, trying not to cry. I

knew he was going to get really angry.

'I mean it, Lizzie. Stop playing with your food and eat it. It's not cheap here, you know.'

I looked across at Mum for help, but she just stared down at her plate. If only she was strong enough to stand up to him for once. 'I'm sorry,' I whispered, 'but I can't eat the fish like this, with the head on and the eye showing. I didn't realize it would come—'

'Oh, for goodness' sake!' Dad leaned over and hacked the head off the fish, shoving it to one side. 'Okay now?'

I nodded, but I still didn't think I could eat it. I nibbled at tiny bits around the edge, trying not to look at the severed head. Dad watched me, his lips set in a straight line. He was always so angry—I couldn't remember the last time I'd seen him laugh or even smile. Bee might have been scared of Melissa Knight, but at least she didn't have to live with her.

He was still in a foul mood the next morning. We were downstairs in the breakfast room and Mum was going on about the memorial for Luke. She wanted him to help her find a suitable place, but it was obvious Dad was fed up with the whole conversation.

'I couldn't go down to the beach for an hour or two, could I?' I said, desperate to get away.

They both glanced up at me, surprised, as if they'd forgotten I was there. 'I won't be long and I've got my phone with me and it's charged up so you can call me. I'll just sit in the shade and read my book. I won't talk to anyone or go off anywhere…'

Dad opened his mouth to say something and

then hesitated for a moment.

'She'll be fine,' said Mum. 'She's been good as gold this past week, keeping herself busy every day.'

'Busy doing what?' said Dad.

'Nothing,' I said, my heart beginning to bang in my chest. 'Just reading and hanging out and—'

'And we went to visit the Tarragona Amphitheatre, didn't we?' said Mum, cutting in. 'That was interesting. Did you know that it held 14,000 people in its day?'

'I'll just go for an hour or so then,' I said, as Mum twittered on about the ruins. I pushed my chair away from the table and started to back out of the room.

'Don't talk to anyone,' warned Dad. 'And don't wander off anywhere. I want you back here at eleven sharp, or there'll be trouble.'

I raced from the hotel down to the beach. I couldn't believe it. I was free! I texted Bee, asking her to meet me, and scrambled up the side of my rock to wait for her. As long as Dad didn't come to check up on me I'd be fine, and even if he did, I could always say I'd just met Bee that morning and that *she* came over to talk to me, not the other way round. How angry could he be about that?

'You made it!' cried Bee a few moments later, running across the beach towards the rock. 'What happened?'

'I don't know,' I yelled. I couldn't stop grinning. 'My mum and dad were talking and they weren't really taking much notice of me and I asked if I could come down for a while and here I am!'

Bee climbed up, plonking herself down next

77

to me. 'I thought I was never going to see you again. Do you think your dad will let you come down every day?'

'Maybe, I'm not sure. It was awful last night— we went to this really posh restaurant and I ordered fish but it came with the head on and eyes still in and it was so gross I couldn't touch it and my dad went mad.'

'What did he do? He didn't force you to eat it, did he?'

'He tried but I walked out of the restaurant.'

Bee looked at me, her eyes huge. 'What, you just got up and walked out? I can't believe it, you're so brave.'

'Not really,' I said, shrugging. 'I mean he couldn't exactly drag me back in, in front of all the other people.'

I wrapped my arms round my knees, staring out to sea. I didn't feel brave at all. I was such a liar, even to Bee. I'd never be able to stand up to Dad like that. I remember Mum telling me once that Luke used to challenge Dad all the time. She said it caused loads of rows, especially during the year before he died. It was probably half the reason Dad was so strict with me.

The memorial was on the last day of the holiday, just five days away, and I still hadn't told Bee about Luke. I wanted to, I wanted to tell her everything—but I didn't want her to know I'd been lying to her, not when she'd trusted me enough to tell me about Melissa Knight and how worried she was that her mum and dad might be splitting up.

*   *   *

It was amazing, but we managed to meet up every morning in the days leading up to the memorial. Mum and Dad were slow to get going in the mornings, so they let me come down to the beach without too much fuss, as long as I kept my phone on and texted them every half an hour. It wasn't as relaxing as before Dad arrived, but it was better than any other time we'd come to Spain.

I actually thought I was going to get away with it—my first normal holiday, hanging out with my first proper friend—but then the day before the memorial, Dad came down to the beach to find me. We were going out somewhere for lunch and he wanted to get an early start. I spotted him just as Bee and I were making our way back from the cafe to our rock.

'Go back over there,' I hissed, pushing Bee in the other direction, trying not to make it too obvious.

She swung round, scared. 'What's the matter? Is it your dad?'

I nodded, turning my back on her and hurrying towards Dad, my heart racing suddenly as he took giant strides towards me across the sand.

'Who was that?' he said as I reached him.

'What do you mean?'

'That girl. Who were you talking to?'

My heart was banging so hard against my chest it hurt. 'No one, I just went to get a drink from the cafe and I was coming straight back. Are we leaving now? Why didn't you text me?'

Dad looked over my head, scanning the beach, his eyes like lasers. 'Come on,' he said finally, 'the restaurant's further away than I thought. Mum's waiting for us in the lobby.'

I didn't dare look round to see where Bee was, but I was sure she'd understand. The whole crazy thing was that she was just the sort of girl Dad would approve of: clever and sensible, never in trouble. He'd probably like her if he met her, but I was too scared to take the chance. She was the best friend I'd ever had and I didn't want to risk losing her, not for anything.

Bee

I nearly died when Lizzie's dad came down to the beach. She shoved me really hard and walked off so quickly that I barely had time to register what was going on. I wanted to grab her and run in the opposite direction, but it all happened too fast. I ducked behind a couple who were just in front of me and watched as Lizzie ran towards him. Her dad was very tall and very fair, like Lizzie. When Lizzie reached him, they spoke for a few moments and then he turned round and strode off, with Lizzie following behind him.

I made my way back to the hotel and found Nan and Mum by the pool. Mum lowered the magazine she was reading as I came towards them. 'I didn't expect to see you back here so soon,' she said, patting the sun lounger for me to sit with her. 'Where's your friend? I was going to ask if she wanted to have lunch with us.'

'She had to go. Her dad came down to get her.'

'Hey, what's the matter?' said Nan, peering at

me over her glasses. 'You've gone white as a sheet.'

'Nothing, Nan, I'm fine, I'm just tired.'

'Oh yes, it's hard work being on holiday,' she joked, chuckling to herself. 'I'm worn out with all this lying around!'

Lizzie texted me later that afternoon. She said they'd had lunch at some posh restaurant miles away and that everything was fine, but then she texted me again to say she had something important to tell me. We arranged to meet straight after breakfast the next morning.

I spent the rest of the afternoon by the pool, hanging out with Mum and Nan. Mum was in quite a good mood. We lay next to each other on the sunbeds and she asked me all about Lizzie and what we'd been doing together. She said it was lovely to see me having such a good time. I came really close to asking her about Dad and if they had split up, but I was scared that if I pushed her too far she might say something I didn't want to hear.

I did ask her about the letters though. I asked if she'd received any more and who they were from. Her mood changed in a flash. She sat up, wrapping her towel round her like a shield. 'I don't want to talk about that,' she said, sounding cross. 'Can't we just enjoy the holiday while we've got the chance?'

'But you've got to tell me,' I said, sitting up as well and grabbing hold of her arm, determined to find out. 'The first letter caused all those rows between you and Dad and now another one's arrived here and you said you'd explain everything to me once we were away. You *promised.*'

Mum bowed her head so I couldn't see her face. 'Look, I've always said that we shouldn't keep secrets, Bee, and I do understand how difficult this

81

is for you, but I just can't talk about it right now. I'm so sorry.'

I didn't know what to say. She really did sound sorry. 'But is everything going to be okay?' was all I managed in the end, my voice breaking.

'Of course it is,' she cried, reaching out for my hand and squeezing it tight. 'Everything's going to be fine, I promise.'

I lay back down, trying not to cry. Another stupid promise she wouldn't keep, but it wasn't as if I could force her to tell me the truth.

*   *   *

I couldn't wait to finish my breakfast the next morning. I barely bothered with anything except a glass of juice and some fruit, but then just as I stood up to leave, Mum said that we were going to a nearby market to buy some presents for her friends at work. I couldn't believe it. I had to meet up with Lizzie. It was the last day of our holiday and my phone was flat so I couldn't even text her to let her know. She'd be waiting for me on the beach. I begged Mum to let me stay back, but she insisted I come with her.

'I don't know why you're making such a fuss,' she said, as we climbed into a taxi outside the hotel. 'We'll be back by lunchtime and anyway, you and Lizzie can stay in touch after the holiday, can't you? It's not as if you're never going to see each other again.'

I stared out of the window, ignoring her. There was no point explaining. She didn't know how lonely I was at Glendale and what a relief it was to meet someone like Lizzie. Someone I could *really* talk to. I'd always been close to Bailey but this was different. Meeting Lizzie was like meeting the one person in the whole world who truly understood me.

The market was in a big square with an old church at one end and a town hall at the other. There were rows and rows of stalls overflowing with fruit and vegetables, hand-crocheted lace tablecloths and the most beautiful stained-glass jewellery. The taxi dropped us off near the church and we joined the crowds of people making their way towards the stalls.

'I don't think I've ever seen so many different olives in my life,' cried Nan, her eyes lighting up. 'And just look at those pastries.' She pushed her way through to the front of the cake stall, waving her arms about and calling out in broken Spanish.

Mum and I left her to it and wandered over to look at the jewellery. I don't usually wear much myself, but I really loved the way the sparkly sea-glass glistened in the sun. I picked up a delicate turquoise necklace. The beads were the exact same colour as Lizzie's eyes.

'Those beads are very precious,' said the man behind the stall. 'Very special beads just for you.'

'Oh, I'd love to get this for Lizzie,' I said, turning to Mum and holding it up to show her. 'It would make such a great leaving present.'

She glanced at the necklace. 'How much is it?'

'Only five euros,' I said, looking at the little ticket attached to the clasp. 'And I'll pay you back, I swear, as soon as we get back. She's going to love it, it's perfect.'

'Not sulking any more then,' Mum teased. She pulled a five euro note out of her purse and was about to hand it to the man when a woman reached over and touched her on the shoulder. She was about Mum's age, pretty, with her hair tied back in a scarf.

'Val?'

Mum turned round slowly, the smile freezing onto her face like a mask.

'I thought it was you. I wasn't sure but...' The woman trailed off. 'How are you, Val?' Her eyes were bright, as if she was trying not to cry.

Mum's mouth moved but no sound came out. She looked around for Nan, but she was still over by the cakes. The woman stared at Mum. Neither of them said anything. I was scared suddenly—I don't know why. It was the silence, the look on Mum's face.

'And this must be Bee,' the woman said finally. 'I can't believe how grown up she is.'

My heart started to thud. How did she know my name? I'd never met her before in my life.

'I'm...I'm sorry,' said Mum, her voice breaking. She dropped the five euro note on the display of necklaces and backed away. 'I'm so sorry, really, but I've...we've...got to go.' She grabbed hold of my hand and pulled me into the crowd.

'*Val!*' The woman's voice rang out after us. '*Please!*'

I looked back. She was still standing there, tears starting to trickle down her face, but Mum began to run, pulling me along, dragging me away from the market. I clutched hold of the turquoise necklace, close to tears myself, worried about Nan and how she was going to find us.

'What's going on?' I shouted. 'Who was that? How do you know her?'

84

'No one,' said Mum. 'I don't know her, it was just a mistake.'

I yanked her arm hard, forcing her to stop. 'Don't be stupid, she knew who I was. *She knew our names!*'

Mum bent over to catch her breath. When she straightened up, she held me by the shoulders, gripping me tight.

'You're right, Bee, I'm sorry. I do know her. She's someone I knew a long time ago, but we fell out. Really badly. It was the shock, that's all, seeing her again after all these years.'

'But why did you fall out? What happened? Is she the person who's been writing to you?'

'Look, we'd better find Nan,' she said, stretching up, trying to spot her over the crowds. 'She'll be over by the food somewhere, wondering where we are. Come on.'

I rubbed my shoulder where Mum's fingers had dug in. How could you fall out with someone that badly?

As soon as we got back to the hotel, Mum disappeared upstairs to her room, complaining of a headache. She'd hardly said a word the whole way back from the market. I'd tried to ask again what was going on, why the woman had been so upset, but Nan had given me a look and changed the subject, nattering on about how many different varieties of olives there were, as if nothing had happened.

I waited until Mum had gone up and then turned to Nan. 'There was this woman by the jewellery stall,' I started. 'She tried to talk to us, she was crying, but Mum just ran off.'

Nan was quiet for a moment as if she was

85

working out what to say—or more likely what *not* to say. 'Your mum's really not herself at the moment, Bee,' she said in the end. 'She's still upset about your dad and what happened before we came away. I wouldn't read too much into it if I was you.'

'Yes, but do *you* know who this woman is? Did she send Mum the letters? Is she the old friend who's been writing to her?'

Nan shook her head, but she didn't quite meet my eye. 'Come on, luvvy, let's go down to the pool. We don't want to miss our last chance to catch the sun.'

Lizzie

Bee came running down to the beach just before twelve. I'd been waiting for ages, terrified that Dad might appear at any moment. It was Luke's memorial at four and I really needed to explain where I was going and why we couldn't spend the rest of the day together. I didn't want the holiday to end without telling her the truth about Luke, however difficult it was.

'I'm so sorry I'm late,' she called out, racing over and clambering up to join me. 'I've had the worst morning. Mum made me go to this market and I couldn't even text you because my phone was dead. Anyway, while we were there, my mum saw a woman she used to know and she totally freaked out. It was awful. The woman was crying and calling out to us and my mum just grabbed me and ran.'

'You're kidding. Who was she?'

'I don't know, Mum wouldn't say, just that they'd fallen out a long time ago. I tried asking my nan but she wouldn't tell me either. I'm sure she's the friend who sent the letters—do you remember, I told you the other day?'

'Yeah, I remember. Maybe she's your dad's ex or something?'

Bee frowned. 'I don't think so somehow...oh, I don't know, I suppose. Anyway, look, I bought you this.'

She pulled something out of her pocket and held it out to show me. It was a delicate turquoise necklace.

'It's a leaving present,' she said. 'I know we're going to see each other again, but it's just so you remember the holiday.'

'Oh, it's beautiful.' I took the necklace carefully and held it up to the sun. 'Look how the light passes through the glass. I'll wear it every single day, I promise. And I'll never, ever forget the holiday.'

I couldn't believe Bee had bought me something so special. I had to tell her the truth. It would be so awful if she found out I'd been lying to her all along before I had the chance to explain properly. I mean what if she ever came over after the holiday and saw photos of Luke plastered all over the walls? She'd never trust me again.

We sat there chatting for a while and then I said I had something to show her. I led her around the bay and over the rocks to the cliffs. We trekked right up to the top, pulling each other along the dusty path. Bee kept moaning that it was too hot and that she wanted to run back down to the sea for a paddle, but I urged her to keep going.

'Finally,' she gasped when we got to the top, flopping down on a rough patch of grass that had grown up between the chalky rocks. 'I can't believe we made it! Have you been up here before?'

'Just once, last year,' I said, flopping down next to her and wrapping my arms round my knees. 'I came up here with my mum when my dad was in one of his foul moods. It's so peaceful, and I love the way the sea sparkles in the sun.'

'It's amazing,' Bee agreed. 'It feels as if we're the only two people in the world.'

We stared out across the sea, quiet for a moment, the sun warming our faces. 'I wish we *were* the only two people in the world,' I said after a bit. I turned to face her, forcing myself to speak. 'Listen, there's something I need to tell you. I should've told you ages ago, right at the start of the holiday, but I didn't know how.'

'But you can tell me anything, Lizzie, you know you can.'

My heart began to beat a bit faster but I forced myself to carry on. 'Do you remember when we were chatting about how much we both loved *Little Women* and I said I was an only child?'

She nodded.

'Well, I was lying. I'm not an only child. Well, I am now, but I used to have an older brother called Luke.'

'What do you mean, *used to*?'

I stared out across the sea. 'He's dead.'

'Oh God, Lizzie. I'm *so* sorry.'

'It's okay, it was years and years ago. I was really young, too young to remember. He was in a car accident, here, in Spain. That's why we come back every year, so my mum and dad can mark the anniversary of his death. We're actually having a special ceremony later this afternoon because it's been ten years since the accident.'

Bee shivered in the heat. 'How awful. What happened?'

I shook my head. 'I don't really know all the details. No one ever talks about it, not properly. There are photos of him everywhere and his room hasn't been touched since he died—but no one will tell me what actually happened.'

'But you must know *something*. Were you in the car?'

I shook my head again. 'We were over here on holiday; it was the first year we came. Luke was hanging out with this boy and they got really drunk one night. And that's when the accident happened.'

'What about the other boy? Did he die as well?'

'No, he survived.'

'Is that why your dad's so strict?'

I glanced down, twisting a blade of grass around my finger. It was hard to explain.

'Yes, but more than just that. It's like he's totally obsessed with keeping me safe. He says Luke got in with a bad crowd at school and that they led him astray, and that's why I have to be homeschooled. I know they must miss him and everything, and that he was their only son, but it's ruining my life. I don't think I can take much more.'

'What do you mean?'

'Dad's just so controlling. And his moods... he's angry all the time. It's like he's got this rage

89

inside, boiling up, ready to explode—and he takes it out on me and Mum. She's scared of him, Bee. We both are, to be honest.'

Bee reached across to give me a hug. 'I don't know what to say. It's so awful. My dad's the total opposite. I don't think I've ever heard him shout at anyone, even when he's arguing with Mum. What's your dad been like since he got here?'

I shrugged. 'Okay, I guess, but it's complicated. He's got other things on his mind this week; he's been distracted. But I'm dreading going home.'

'Isn't there someone you could talk to? Someone who could help?'

'No one would understand. No one knows the whole story. You're the only person I've ever told. The only person I've ever trusted enough.'

I lay back in the grass, staring up at the sky. I was relieved I'd told Bee the truth, but it didn't really change anything. 'I wish we could stay up here for ever. Something happened to my dad the day my brother died. It's like his heart froze over. I know it sounds terrible but I wish I never had to see him again in my life.'

*   *   *

The ceremony for Luke came round all too soon. Mum had found this shady, wooded area about ten minutes' drive from the hotel. She said we'd had a picnic there the day before Luke died and that it was one of her happiest memories of us all together. Apparently Luke had kept me entertained for ages by putting slices of orange in his mouth, skin side out, and then smiling, so that it looked as if he had an orange smile.

'You were squealing with laughter,' she said, as we set off from the hotel. 'You kept saying, "Orange mouth again, Lukie! Orange mouth again!"'

'Is that what I called him then?' I asked. A funny feeling washed over me. Not a memory exactly, just a weird sense that I'd seen a boy with a segment of orange in his mouth—but I couldn't say where or when or if it was even Luke.

'We *all* did,' said Mum quietly. 'He was our Lukie.' Her eyes filled with tears and she turned to stare out of the window. She'd been crying ever since I got back to the hotel. Dad said she'd had a bad morning and that the sooner the ceremony was over the better. He was driving along now, his face set like stone. He never joined in with Mum's memories of Luke.

The wooded area was completely deserted. Mum led us through to a small clearing and laid out some blankets. I wondered if she'd come here earlier in the week to make sure it was secluded enough. It wasn't as if we could hold a private ceremony with loads of other people hanging around.

'I've brought a candle and some music,' she said. 'But that's all really. I just wanted us to be together, to mark the day.' Tears started to run down her face. 'I know they say time's a great healer but sometimes I don't think I'll ever stop missing him...'

'This really isn't helping!' snapped Dad. His voice sounded even louder than usual in the silence of the wood. 'I thought you said you

91

wanted to mark the day in a *positive* way. Isn't that what you said?'

'Please, Michael. Don't shout at me, not today. It's not just the anniversary…'

'What?' I said. 'What else is it?'

Mum and Dad glanced at each other. 'It's nothing,' sniffed Mum. 'Just something that happened earlier. Have *you* brought anything for the ceremony, Lizzie?'

I shook my head.

'But I thought you said you were going to write a few words…'

'No, Mum! *You* said I was going to write a few words—I never said I was going to write anything. Can we just go back to the hotel? This is creeping me out.'

'Don't be so selfish,' snapped Dad. But he looked as if he wished he could go as well.

Mum put her hands over her ears. 'Can you both just be quiet, *please,* for *one* afternoon! That's not too much to ask, is it?'

She took the candle out of her bag, her hand trembling as she held a lit match to the wick. The flame flickered and went out. She tried again, striking another match, and then another. 'I've brought some photos with me,' she said, when the candle was finally lit. 'Some photos from that holiday…'

There was a moment's silence and then Dad swiped at the bag, knocking it out of Mum's hands. 'No!' he barked. 'I've had enough! I don't want to look at any bloody photos! It's been ten years, for Christ's sake. I can't do this any more, Val, we've got to move on.' He jumped up and walked off into the trees, his shoulders hunched up around his ears.

Mum watched him go, her face crumbling. 'I really wanted you to prepare something, Lizzie,' she said, turning to look at me. 'Something small, *anything*, just to mark the day.'

'I am marking the day. I'm here, aren't I?' I wanted to make her finally realize what this was all like for me, but I felt so guilty at the same time. 'I wish you'd just leave me out of it.'

'What do you mean?' she cried. 'Luke was your brother!'

'I know,' I said. 'I know he was my brother and I wish he was here. I wish he'd never been involved in the accident. I wish we'd never come to Spain that year. I wish I could remember him. I could wish and wish until I burst, but it's not going to make the slightest difference, is it?'

I got up and stalked off after Dad. I couldn't bear to sit there with her for another minute. She called out after me, but I ignored her, walking deeper into the wood. I'd known the ceremony was going to be a nightmare. I'd been dreading it so much, ever since she first mentioned it. She was just so obsessed with Luke.

I heard Dad before I saw him. He was making the most terrible noise, moaning and gasping as if he couldn't breathe. I went a few steps further and saw him up ahead, leaning against a tree. He was bent over, tears streaming down his face. I stopped where I was, my stomach twisting up. I felt scared suddenly. I'd never seen him cry before. He was always throwing his weight about, shouting and carrying on, but I'd never seen him cry.

I turned and ran back to Mum without stopping.

'We've really got to go, like *right now*,' I said. 'I'm sorry about Luke, I really am. I didn't mean to be so horrible. I wish I could miss him. I wish I could remember him, even a little bit, but please, Mum, can we just go?'

She must have caught something in my voice. She got up and pulled me into her arms. 'No, *I'm* sorry, Lizzie. This is all such a mess and it's not your fault. None of it's your fault. You really don't need to apologize. And yes, we can leave as soon as Dad comes back.' She stroked my hair and I leaned against her, my eyes closed tight, trying to block out the awful memory of Dad by the tree.

Bee

Lizzie and I said goodbye later that night. We'd arranged to meet at Lizzie's hotel after dinner, but Mum didn't want me to go. She said she didn't want me to leave the hotel until the morning. She was still upset about the woman in the marketplace, but she refused to discuss it with me or tell me why.

'But I've got to say goodbye,' I said, desperate to make her understand. 'It will break Lizzie's heart if I don't show up.'

Mum shook her head, her lips set in that awful straight line. I felt like telling her about Lizzie's brother dying so she'd realize how important it was. Lizzie had confided in me, trusted me with her deepest secrets, which was more than could be said for Mum.

'You spent hours with her this afternoon, Bee, and you haven't even finished packing.'

'I couldn't care less about packing! I promised Lizzie I'd go and if I don't show up she'll think I don't care.'

'Lizzie *again*! Honestly, Bee, it's not as if you're going to see her after the holiday. Can you please just get on with your packing? You've been running free all holiday, but it's over now.'

'What do you mean? Of course I'm going to see her again—you said so yourself when we were in the taxi this morning. And anyway, she's my best friend.'

Mum opened her mouth and closed it again, as if she was about to say something; something about Lizzie. She sank down on the edge of the bed. 'We never should've come,' she muttered. 'Dad was right. It was so stupid.'

'I'll take Bee to the hotel,' said Nan quietly. 'Don't worry. We'll go and come straight back. It's only right that she should have the chance to say goodbye.'

I didn't like the way Nan said that—it sounded so final—but I bolted out of the door before Mum could change her mind or stop us. It was obvious that the letters and the woman in the marketplace, and maybe even the sudden holiday to Spain, were all connected in some way—if only I could work out how and why Mum was in such a state about it.

Lizzie was waiting for me just inside the entrance of her big, swanky hotel. I pushed my way through the revolving doors, relieved to see her. 'Sorry I'm late; my mum didn't want me to come. She was still upset about that woman she saw in the market this morning.'

95

'Did she tell you who she was? What did she say?'

I shrugged. 'She didn't say anything. Why, what's the matter?'

She seemed nervous, scared even. Her eyes were bright with tears.

'Nothing. I'm fine, really. I just don't want to say goodbye.'

'I know; me neither. How was the ceremony? For your brother?'

'Terrible. Worse than I could've imagined. Listen, Bee...' She looked round suddenly. A man was walking towards us across the marble floor. It was her dad—I recognized him from the beach. Lizzie tensed up as he reached us. 'This is my dad,' she muttered. 'Dad, this is my friend Bee.'

Lizzie's dad nodded at me, but he didn't say anything. His eyes were the same turquoise blue as Lizzie's, but cold. I shivered slightly, remembering what Lizzie had said earlier in the day.

'Look, I've got to go,' she said, throwing her arms round my neck and dissolving into tears. 'Promise you won't forget me, Bee. Promise you'll still be my friend. Whatever happens...'

'Of course I will, and I'll never forget you. We'll see each other in a couple of weeks, max, and I'll call you as soon as I get back. We might even see each other tomorrow at the airport.'

She clung onto me, her cheek wet against mine, but her dad pulled her away.

'It's time to go, Lizzie. Come on.'

I called out to her as he dragged her towards the lift. 'I'll phone you...I'll speak to you soon, Lizzie... Don't forget me...' She looked back over her shoulder, her eyes wide. I got the strongest feeling she was trying to tell me something. Something important.

'What?' I mouthed, but she gave a last helpless shrug as they stepped into the dark of the lift and the doors slid closed behind them.

Lizzie

It was the necklace that sparked everything off. I'd hidden it in my case when I got back from my clifftop talk with Bee, but later on, after the ceremony, Mum decided to help me finish packing. She'd stopped crying, finally, and seemed to be feeling calmer, but then she turned to face me suddenly, the necklace in her hand.

'What's this?' she said, holding it up to show me. Her face was white, her eyes huge in her face.

'Erm, someone gave it to me,' I said. My face started to burn up. I don't know why—it wasn't as if I'd done anything wrong.

Mum looked around to see if Dad was listening, but he was in the bathroom. He'd been locked in there ever since we got back.

'Who gave it to you, Lizzie? I want you to tell me right now.'

I stared at her. She looked scared. Why was she reacting like this?

'My friend, Bee.'

'Bee?' Mum sank down onto the bed. 'Your *friend* Bee?'

'Yes, my friend Bee. What's the big deal?' I grabbed the necklace out of her hand and stuffed

97

it back in my case.

'I'm sorry, Lizzie, but you can't be friends with Bee,' said Mum slowly.

Our eyes locked. 'What are you talking about?' I said. 'I *am* friends with her. And why are you saying it like that? As if you *know* her?'

'As if you know who?' said Dad, coming out of the bathroom at the worst possible moment.

'Bee,' said Mum faintly. 'She knows Bee.'

'Of course I know Bee. She's my best friend. Stop talking about her like that.'

Mum shook her head, her eyes filling with tears.

'Oh, Mum, *please* can you just talk to me without crying?'

'Be quiet!' said Dad. 'I want to know exactly what's been going on.' He grabbed my arm and yanked me over to where he was standing. 'How do you know Bee? Where did you meet her?'

'Dad, you're hurting me!' I pulled my arm away. 'I met her on the beach. We're friends, okay. We've been meeting up every day, but don't worry, she's perfectly respectable and—'

'And what about her mother and father?' snapped Dad, interrupting me. 'Have you met them as well? Do they know who you are?'

I shook my head. 'Her dad's not with them, she's here with her mum and her nan. I've seen them a couple of times—her nan's always by the pool—but I haven't met them, not properly.'

I looked at Mum. She was sobbing, her shoulders shaking. 'What's going on?' I said, beginning to feel scared. 'Why are you so upset?'

Dad leaned down to me so that our faces were almost touching. 'Why didn't you tell us you'd met someone on the beach? We *trusted* you.'

'I told Mum. She knew I'd made friends with someone, but I didn't tell you because of *this*. Because you *always* react like this.'

Dad breathed in through his nose, as if he was trying to control himself. 'You're not to see Bee again. Not ever. You're not to see her or speak to her or make contact with her in any way. Do you understand me?' His eyes were icy slits.

'No, I don't understand,' I said, twisting away, tears springing to my eyes. 'I don't understand anything. Why can't I see her again? We're supposed to be saying goodbye later tonight. She's coming here after dinner.'

Dad raised his hand as if he was going to hit me. I shrank back towards Mum. *'She's not coming here!'* he roared. *'She's not coming. Do you hear me?'*

I stepped back further and cuddled up next to Mum on the bed, trying not to cry. 'Just to say goodbye,' I whispered. 'Please. I won't see her again, I swear, but please just let me say goodbye.'

Mum squeezed my hand. 'We should let them say goodbye,' she said, looking through her tears at Dad. 'You can go down with her. It's not their fault. They're not to blame.'

'Can't you just tell me what's going on?' I said, really scared now. 'We're not to blame for what? Why can't I be friends with Bee?'

Suddenly something clicked in my brain. It was like the last piece of a puzzle slotting into place.

'You're the woman in the market, aren't you?' I said to Mum. 'You *know* Bee's mum. You saw them buying the necklace.' It had to be her.

There was no other explanation. Somehow she knew Bee's mum.

Mum grasped my hand. 'I'm sorry, Lizzie, I'm so sorry.'

'But I don't understand. How do you know her? And why did she run away from you in the market?'

Dad walked towards me, furious. *'Why did she run away?'* he yelled, his face almost purple with rage. *'I'll tell you why she ran away!'*

*   *   *

I couldn't take it in. Dad stood there, repeating it over and over, but it couldn't be true. It had to be a mistake. I put my hands over my ears, but he pulled them away, forcing me to listen. It was like being trapped in a nightmare. I watched his lips move but the words didn't make any sense. I turned to Mum, pleading with her to make him stop.

I don't know how she did it, but she somehow convinced him to let me go down to the lobby for five minutes. She said I needed to say goodbye to Bee, to have some 'closure', as she put it, but then I'd have to accept that the friendship was over. For ever.

Dad didn't say a word in the lift, he stared straight ahead, his eyes flat. I don't think he had any intention of letting me talk to Bee on my own, but as we were passing the front desk one of the receptionists called out to him—something to do with an alarm call for the morning. I slipped away, dashing over to the doors. There was no sign of her yet, but I knew she'd come.

She arrived a few moments later, pushing her way through the revolving doors. Her nan was with her, but she waited outside, watching Bee through the big glass windows. I glanced back towards Dad, but he was still talking to the hotel receptionist.

'Sorry I'm late,' she said. Then she told me her mum was still upset about the incident in the market.

Nervously, I looked back again. Dad would be over any second.

'What's the matter?' said Bee.

'Nothing. I'm fine, really. I just don't want to say goodbye.' She didn't seem to have any idea what was going on between our mums. I had to tell her. I had to explain—but it wasn't something you could just blurt out. I heard Dad's shoes on the marble floor. It was too late. He was coming towards us.

'This is my dad,' I muttered, as he reached us. 'Dad, this is my friend Bee.'

He looked at her as if she was evil. As if *she* was to blame.

'Look, I've got to go,' I said, throwing my arms round her. 'Promise you won't forget me, Bee. Promise you'll still be my friend. Whatever happens...'

She didn't understand—how could she? I tried one more time to make her realize there was something important she should know, as Dad dragged me away.

'What?' she mouthed, but I could only shrug back. It was hopeless. Dad was holding onto me, pulling me towards the open lift. I'd just have to think of another way to let her know. Another way

to tell her the terrible truth. I still couldn't believe it *was* the truth, but Dad's words were etched on my brain like an ugly tattoo:
    'BEE'S DAD KILLED LUKE!'

Bee

I sat up in bed for ages, too confused about everything to sleep. Why was Lizzie so scared? What had she been trying to tell me? I couldn't bear to see her so distressed. Something must have happened at the ceremony for her brother. I had a horrible feeling she was in trouble and there was nothing I could do to help her.

Nan could see how upset I was when I came out of the hotel. I told her what had happened and begged her to go back in with me to make sure Lizzie was okay, but she said it wasn't really our place to interfere. She said we had to leave Lizzie and her family to sort things out for themselves. But how are you supposed to turn your back on your best friend just when she needs you most?

When we got back to the room, Mum seemed a bit calmer. She gave me a cuddle and said she was sorry she'd got so cross. I asked her about the letters and the woman in the marketplace and why they'd fallen out so badly, but she wouldn't say.

'It's much too late to get into a big discussion about that now,' she sighed, pulling me tighter and stroking my hair. 'Not when we've got such an early start in the morning.'

It was so frustrating. I didn't want a big

102

discussion; I just wanted her to tell me what was going on. I gave up in the end and went to my room.

I was so desperate to talk to Lizzie. I needed to make sure she was okay, and find out what she'd been trying to tell me. Mum might have been keeping secrets, but best friends tell each other everything.

To take my mind off things, I reached under my pillow for my literacy book. I hadn't written a word of my poetry project yet; I'd been far too busy having fun. But suddenly I knew exactly what my theme was going to be. It was so obvious. I plugged my phone in to recharge, picked up a pen and turned to a clean page.

Lizzie

I thought of swapping the suitcases later that night after saying goodbye to Bee. Mum and Dad were asleep and I was sitting up in bed, writing my diary, trying to make sense of everything. I scribbled away, pouring it all out, until I was so tired it was impossible to keep my eyes open. It felt important to write down every last word—but I still couldn't believe it was true. How could Bee's dad be responsible for Luke's death?

Mum had tried to explain. She said our families had been close friends and that it had been a terrible, tragic accident, but Dad wouldn't have it. He insisted Bee's dad was to blame—that it was murder, plain and simple. I didn't say anything at all. I was too shocked. I tried to remember what

Bee had said about her dad, something about how he never got angry, or lost his temper. He certainly didn't sound like a murderer.

When I was too exhausted to write another word, I locked my diary and leaned down to tuck it right at the bottom of my case. I wanted to talk to Bee, to tell her what was going on, but Dad had confiscated my phone and deleted all her contact details. I had to find some way to get in touch with her. Some way to explain. And that's when the idea came to me.

Bee and I had identical suitcases, except for one crucial difference—she had a purple label attached to hers with her name written across it in bright blue marker pen. I remember her showing it to me when I picked up the wrong case on the first day of the holiday. So if I could somehow get to the baggage reclaim area before she did when we arrived back in London, I could grab her case, remove the label, and take it home.

That was the first part of the plan, the easy part. But it would only work if she then took my suitcase home instead of hers, by mistake, just like Mum did all those years ago. *My* suitcase, with *my* diary hidden at the bottom—explaining everything that had happened and why I was never allowed to see her again.

Bee

The journey home was a nightmare. Mum said she'd been up all night and even Nan seemed on edge. I was really hoping we'd bump into Lizzie at the airport, but it was so crowded and there were so many different queues, it was impossible to know if she was there or not. I thought I caught a glimpse of her dad at one point, queuing up at a cashpoint, but I hid behind Nan, scared he might turn round and see me.

I was so certain she'd been trying to tell me something the night before at the hotel. She'd been about to say something before her dad came over. If only he'd left us on our own for a few more minutes. It was awful seeing her so upset. I remembered what she'd said about him being angry all the time, ready to explode.

I tried talking to Mum again once we were up in the air, determined to find out about the woman in the market. And finally, she started to tell me. She said the woman's name was Suzie and that they'd been best friends; that our two families had been really close. But then she started to cry.

'It's so difficult to explain, Bee.' She reached into her bag for a tissue. 'It was such a long time ago. I've tried to put it behind me, but this holiday, being in Spain, it's just been so...' By then she was crying too hard to carry on.

'Leave it, Bee,' warned Nan. 'You can see how upset she is.'

Mum was breathing very fast, her eyes wide with fright.

'Come on, Val, calm down,' soothed Nan. 'Look into my eyes. Now, deep breath in, deep breath out, deep breath in, deep breath out.' She cupped Mum's face in her hands, breathing with her, until Mum's breathing slowed down.

'I'm sorry,' I muttered. 'I didn't mean to upset you.' I'd never seen Mum like this before. She's not exactly the emotional type. I couldn't even remember the last time I saw her cry before Dad went missing and all of this started.

'I just don't know why I came,' she said to Nan, when she'd recovered enough to speak again. 'I wish I'd listened to Phillip. Why don't I ever listen to him?'

Nan shook her head. 'You just thought it was time to move on, we both did. To finally lay things to rest.'

'Lay *what* things to rest?' I said. 'This is crazy. When are you going to tell me what's going on? Is it the lady in the market—*Suzie*—is she the reason Dad didn't want to come to Spain? *Who is she really?*' But Mum's eyes filled up again and she fumbled about in her bag for a fresh tissue.

I gave up after that but I watched her carefully. This wasn't just some row with an old friend— it was obviously far more serious than that. It was almost as if someone had kidnapped my calm, sensible mum and put this new hysterical, worked-up person in her place. I sat back in my seat, more frightened and confused than ever. But as the plane came in to land I made a promise to myself: I was going to find out what was in those letters if it was the last thing I did.

Lizzie

It was chaos at the airport. I didn't see Bee until we were about to board. She was way ahead of us in the queue, but when we got on the plane I spotted her nan lifting a plastic carrier bag into the overhead storage area right at the back. I didn't know why they'd chosen to sit there, but hopefully it meant I'd be able to get to the baggage reclaim carousel before they did.

I couldn't think of anything else as the plane took off. It felt weird to be so close to Bee but not say hello or talk to her or anything, especially after finding out something so shocking. I was praying with all my heart that Dad had got it wrong. Maybe there were two girls called Bee, two different families? I couldn't bear to think of Bee's family linked to ours in such a horrible way.

*   *   *

We were one of the first in the queue for passport control when we arrived in London, I made sure of that. I kept looking behind me, expecting Bee and her mum and nan to appear, but there was no sign of them. The man inside the little booth seemed to be taking ages, much longer than usual, turning each page of our passports in slow motion. I willed him to hurry up, desperate to put my plan into action.

As soon as we were through, I raced on ahead. I knew exactly where to go; I'd been there so many times before. I stood in front of the huge baggage reclaim board to see which carousel we needed. Our flight number was up there— and our arrival time—but the space where the carousel number should have been was blank. I kept my eyes glued to the board. I didn't dare look behind me in case I saw Bee and her family approaching. Every time the board updated, my stomach lurched. Where was the number? Where *was it*? How could it take so long?

Mum and Dad caught up with me. Dad was distracted, on the phone to someone from work.

'I think I'll just nip to the loo to freshen up,' said Mum. 'I always feel a bit grubby after flying.'

'Okay,' I said, trying to keep my voice even. 'I'll see you at the carousel.'

I felt like I was on some sort of secret mission, but swapping the cases was the only way to make sure Bee found out what was really going on. I stared back up at the board. Still blank… still blank…*still blank*… And then suddenly it was there. Carousel 8. I turned and raced down the escalator. Dad followed behind me, peeling off at the bottom to grab a trolley.

The bags started to come round quite quickly. It didn't take long for Bee's to appear—or was it mine? It was impossible to tell. A moment later, an identical case appeared. Two bright pink cases covered in big purple flowers. They were both coming round the carousel at more or less the same time. I squeezed right through to the front as the first of the two cases trundled towards me. I could see the label as clear as anything—*BEE BROOKS*, written in bright blue marker pen.

I reached out, desperately hoping that Bee was

still queuing up at passport control or getting a trolley. My hand closed around the handle and in one swift movement I pulled it towards me, ripped off the label and set it down at my feet. Dad was standing right next to me, but he was too busy grabbing his case in one hand and Mum's in the other to notice what I was up to. I hauled Bee's case onto the trolley, my heart going a million miles a minute, and looked round for Mum.

I felt as if every nerve in my body was screaming out. Where was she? How long could it take to freshen up? Any second now Bee would arrive at the carousel and realize I'd taken her case. A trickle of cold sweat ran down my back. I scanned the crowds for Mum, willing her to appear, cursing her for being so slow.

By the time she finally came out of the loo I was in a total state. We made our way out of the airport and towards the car park. I'd done it. I had Bee's suitcase, which meant, fingers crossed, she'd soon be on her way home with mine. The only thing I had to hope for now—was that she'd find my diary. And read it.

Bee

When we finally landed in England, Mum refused point-blank to get off the plane. She said she wasn't feeling well and that she couldn't face the crowds. I tried to help her out of her seat but she started to breathe very fast again, her eyes wide with fear. I didn't know what to do; I was scared she was going to be sick or pass out.

Nan called the stewardess over to explain and asked if we could wait until everyone had left the plane. The stewardess was really kind. She brought Mum a glass of water and joked that she'd never had a passenger who was too scared to get *off* the plane before. She crouched down in front of Mum and talked to her in a really calm voice until her breathing slowed down again.

I had no idea if Lizzie was on the plane or not. We were right at the back, but it was impossible to see down the aisle because the stewardess was blocking my view. By the time Mum felt well enough to get off, and we'd made our way through passport control and down to the baggage reclaim area, there were only our three cases left, piled up at the side of the carousel. Nan went over to get them while I waited with Mum. If Lizzie and her parents *had* been on our flight, they were long gone.

Mum and Nan sat in silence more or less the whole way back from the airport. Mum was calm again, but she looked so pale and worn out you'd never have believed she'd just spent two weeks in the sun. I just wished she could trust me enough to tell me what was really going on and why she was in such a terrible state.

The closer we got to home, the more I started to think about Dad and whether he'd be there, waiting for us. I suddenly missed him so much it was like a pain deep inside my heart. I needed to see him so badly, to tell him how upset Mum was and to beg him to come home and make everything okay again.

Lizzie

I started to pick holes in my plan as soon as we left the airport. It was never going to work. Just because I'd taken Bee's case, it didn't necessarily mean that she'd take mine. She'd probably notice there was no label as soon as she pulled my suitcase off the carousel, and if she opened it right there and then to check, and saw it was mine, she'd just assume I'd taken hers by mistake. She'd have no way of knowing I'd done it on purpose.

I half-thought about telling Mum and trying to get her to contact Bee for me, but I knew she'd be far too scared to go behind Dad's back. She'd attempted to talk to him at the airport—something about moving forward, trying to find a way to forgive, but he'd told her to drop it. He said the holiday was over and he didn't want to hear Bee or her family mentioned ever again.

Bee

We caught a bus from the tube station and then dragged our cases down the street. The house was waiting for us, dark and silent. I could tell before we even went in that Dad wasn't there, but I still couldn't stop myself from calling his name as we went through the front door. A wave of disappointment washed over me. Mum went straight upstairs to lie down, while Nan bustled around, turning on lights, and tidying up the pile of letters and flyers by the front door.

'Who's for a cuppa?' she trilled, doing her best to sound cheery. 'Bee?'

'No thanks, Nan, I'm going upstairs to unpack. I'll have something later.'

She stopped sorting through the mail for a moment and looked up. 'Can we have a little chat before you go up, Bee? It won't take two secs.'

'You're not cross with me, are you?' I asked, remembering how she'd snapped at me on the plane.

'Don't be silly, why on earth would I be cross with you? You haven't done anything wrong.'

I waited until she'd made a pot of tea and we sat at the kitchen table.

'It was a great holiday, wasn't it?' she said, lifting her cup to take a sip. 'You did enjoy yourself, didn't you?'

'Of course I did, I had a brilliant time. But I can't stop thinking about Mum and Dad and the letters and the woman in the market and whether Dad's going to come home.'

Nan sighed. 'That's what I wanted to talk to you about, actually.'

I leaned forward. 'But I thought you didn't know who she was.'

'I do know her, Bee.' Nan looked a bit embarrassed. 'I'm sorry I didn't tell you before. I think I was in a state of shock. Suzie and your mum were friends a long time ago, when you were a baby.'

'I know, Nan, she told me that on the plane. But I want to know why they fell out, why Mum ran away like that. And why did she start staying stuff about Lizzie when we were packing—about not seeing her again? What's Lizzie got to do with any of this?'

'Well, the thing is,' said Nan, 'the woman in the market, Suzie…she's *Lizzie's* mum.'

I stared at Nan as if she was speaking a foreign language. 'What do you mean? *My friend* Lizzie? That was her mum?'

'You see we didn't put two and two together—not straight away,' said Nan. 'We always knew Suzie's daughter as Elizabeth, not Lizzie, so when you said you'd made friends with a girl called *Lizzie,* it didn't occur to us that it might be the same girl. It sounds silly, I know, but we hadn't seen them for ten years.'

'But didn't you recognize her? You saw us together nearly every day.'

'The last time I saw her she wasn't even three and she's practically a teenager now! I did think there was something familiar about her, but you know what I'm like, my brain's not as sharp as it once was! It was only when Mum bumped into Suzie in the market that it all began to slot into place.'

My head felt as if it was going to burst. It was too much to take in. 'So was it Suzie who sent the letters to Mum? Is that why Mum wanted to go to Spain?'

Nan nodded.

'So you mean I already *knew* Lizzie before I met her on the beach.' I scraped back my chair, pushing away from the table. 'I've got to speak to Mum. Why did they fall out, Nan? What happened? And what was in the first letter? Why was Dad so angry? Why didn't he want to come to Spain with us?

None of it makes any sense.'

'Just wait a second, Bee.' Nan got up and came round the table. 'I don't think your mum can handle talking about it right now. She's *really* upset. More upset than you realize.'

'But I need to know. It's so obvious it's all connected: Lizzie's mum, and Dad going to stay at Uncle Ron's and the letters.' I paused for a moment, thinking, desperately trying to tie all the threads together. 'Did Dad have an affair with Suzie?' I said after a bit, praying I was wrong. 'Were they together? Is that what the letters were about?'

'What do you mean, an affair?' cried Nan. 'It was nothing like that!'

'Well, what was it then? You can't keep it from me for ever. I've got a right to know.'

Nan looked at me for a long time without saying anything.

'Your mum will tell you, Bee, trust me. But you'll have to wait until she's ready. Don't rush her, please. It won't help.'

I shook my head, so frustrated I wanted to scream. 'But when? When's she going to tell me? And what about my dad? When do you think he'll come home? I really need to talk to him.'

Nan smiled, but she looked worried. 'Soon, my love. Really soon.'

*   *   *

It felt weird to be back in my room. We'd only been away for two weeks but it felt more like two years. Two weeks ago, I was poor old bullied Bee, but not any more. For the first time in my life, I had a proper best friend and everything was going to be

114

different. Lizzie might not go to my school, but just knowing she was my friend made me feel stronger and more confident than before.

I'd texted her on the way home from the airport but she hadn't texted back yet. I tried ringing but there was a weird tone, as if the phone was broken or out of service. We were supposed to be making plans to meet up later in the week. I knew we'd only just said goodbye, but I needed to tell her about our mums and the fact that they used to be friends, and ask her if she knew what was going on. Maybe that was what she'd been trying to tell me before her dad dragged her into the lift at the hotel.

I hauled my case onto my bed and unzipped it. I was planning to sort my stuff out and then pop round to Bailey's to see how his camping trip had turned out. I'd texted him in the car on the way back from the airport to say we were home. I couldn't wait to tell him about meeting Lizzie and the caves and the creepy message carved into the wall. It was just the sort of thing he'd love.

I opened my case and glanced down. Something was wrong. For a second, I thought I was seeing things. I closed my eyes tight and then opened them again. My clothes weren't in there, or my books or any of my stuff. There must have been a mistake; a mix-up at the airport. There were some denim shorts lying across the top and an old straw sun hat. And tucked into a pocket in the lining was a delicate, turquoise-blue necklace.

I scooped it out and sat there, clutching the necklace close to my heart.

It wasn't my case at all.

It was Lizzie's.

Lizzie

It was weird being home. It felt as if everything had changed. I really needed to talk to Bee, to tell her what Dad had said about *her* dad killing Luke—to find out if it was true, if she knew anything—but I literally had no way of contacting her. Dad was determined to keep us apart at all costs. He'd confiscated my phone and wouldn't let me use his laptop. It was a nightmare. I didn't know where she lived or how to let her know I was still her friend.

I hauled her case upstairs, wondering when I should mention to Mum that I'd brought the wrong one home by mistake. I'd have to tell her sooner or later because she'd want to know where all my stuff was. I felt like giving up. My case was most likely dumped in lost property somewhere at the airport—and even if Bee *had* taken it home and read my diary, she'd still have no way of getting in touch with me.

Her suitcase was much neater than mine, all her clothes neatly folded under a layer of books. I don't know why I opened it really; it wasn't as if I was looking for anything in particular. Most of the books were novels, but nestled amongst them was a blue exercise book, the kind you use when you go to a proper school.

I stared at it, my heart starting to thump. It was Bee's literacy book, her poetry project—her summer holiday homework. I remembered her saying in the cave that she had to pick a theme and write a series of poems and now her book was here, in my bedroom. I flicked through, wondering if she'd actually written any poems, as she'd never mentioned it again while we were away.

I found them right at the back of the book. Three poems under the word *FRIENDSHIP!*

The Friendship Rock
The friendship rock where I met Lizzie
Her hair straight and my hair frizzy
A special place to sit and share
To laugh and cry and trust and care
To form a bond so deep and true
To know each other through and through
The friendship rock where I met Lizzie
Her hair straight and my hair frizzy.

I read it again, smiling. It was such a lovely poem. I could almost see us sitting up on our rock in the sunshine. But the next poem was completely different.

Being Me
Be different!
Be quiet!
Be scared!
Be small!
Be someone else, or not at all!

That's the way it used to be,
That's the way they made me feel.
I was weak and they were strong,
They were right and I was wrong.

That's the way it *used* to be,
That's the way they made me feel.
That's the way it was before,
But not any more…

Poor Bee. I knew she was unhappy at school and that she was being bullied, but I didn't realize it was as bad as that. I was itching to find Melissa Knight and make her feel as small and insignificant as she'd made Bee feel. I wanted to shove the poem right in her face so she could see what she'd been doing.

The third poem was called 'Goodbye'.

Goodbye
Pale face
Scared eyes
Deep fears
Hope dies
Tight hug
Something's wrong
Last shrug
Stay strong
Hot tears
Holiday's end
Take care
Best friend.

I glanced back up to the top of the page. There was a date: *Friday 8th August*. She'd written the poems yesterday. Last night, after we'd said goodbye. I ran my fingers over the words, shivering. Bee had been having such a hard time at school, and now she'd think I'd dropped her too. I felt really weird about what Bee's dad was supposed to have done, but I didn't want her to think I didn't care enough to get in touch with her again.

I paced around for a bit, desperately trying to make sense of it all. Dad had made it sound so straightforward. Bee's dad had killed Luke, so Bee and I were never allowed to see each other again. End of. But something had been niggling away at the back of my mind. It was something Mum had said when she was trying to explain everything to me—about our two families being really close friends once and spending lots of time together.

If that was true—if our family *had* been close friends with Bee's family—then Bee and I must've known each other when we were little girls. Maybe we were friends. Maybe we were even *best* friends. It was difficult to believe, but in some ways it made perfect sense. The way we just clicked; the fact that we got on so well.

I wracked my brains. If only I could remember. I wanted to know what we were like back then. What we got up to together, and what happened when it ended. How did Mum explain the fact that both Luke *and* Bee had disappeared out of my life? There was so much I didn't understand. So much I needed to know. Was this why Mum and Dad had never told me much about the night Luke died? Because their close friends were involved? I just couldn't believe it was true.

*   *   *

Mum called me down for dinner just before seven. She'd made an omelette and chips, but I said I wasn't hungry.

'Come on, Lizzie, you've hardly eaten a thing all day. I know you've had a shock, but you can't starve yourself.'

'Where's Dad? Isn't he eating with us?'

Mum's eyes darted to the door. 'He's upstairs, catching up on his emails. He's very upset about everything.'

He's not the only one, I felt like saying.

I wasn't ready to ask her about Bee yet, or about what had really happened when we were little girls. Maybe I was scared she'd say something that might change the way I felt about Bee and our friendship, convince me that what Dad said was true. 'I'm sorry but I've brought the wrong suitcase home by mistake,' I said instead.

Mum stopped dishing up. 'What do you mean?'

'Well, it looks like my case, it's exactly the same, but it's got someone else's stuff in it.'

'But there must be a label. A name or address.'

I shook my head. There was no way I was going to tell her it was Bee's. 'I've looked through, but there's nothing; just clothes and some books.'

Mum sighed and then carried on serving up the dinner. 'We'll have to ring the airline; explain what's happened and see if your case is still at the airport somewhere.'

She plonked the plate down in front of me and started to rummage through her bag. 'I've got the number in here somewhere, but it'll be a miracle if someone actually picks up, especially this late. We'll probably have to sort it out tomorrow.'

I left her hanging on the phone and went back upstairs. I was intending to go straight to bed, but something led me to Luke's room. It was weird,

120

as if I suddenly had no control over my feet. I stood in the doorway, my palms slick with sweat. I wanted to find out more about my big brother and what happened to him, but I was scared. It felt wrong, somehow, as if I was meddling in something that was none of my business.

I stood there for a bit, a sad feeling settling over me like a heavy coat, and then Mum called up the stairs. 'Come and eat your dinner, Lizzie. Hurry up, please, it's getting cold.'

'Coming,' I said. But all I could think about was Luke, and Bee, and Bee's dad and the accident, and all the unanswered questions about that night that were whirling around inside my head. Mum would just have to wait. I wiped my hands on my jeans, stepped into Luke's room and closed the door behind me.

Bee

I sat there, clutching the necklace, trying to understand. Mum, Nan and I had been the last passengers off the plane and through security. Our cases were the only three left by the time we got to the carousel. I'd noticed the label was missing on mine when we got out of the taxi but I'd just assumed it got torn off during the journey.

So did that mean Lizzie had taken my case home instead of hers? I knew she'd pulled my case off the carousel when we *arrived* in Spain, but surely she wouldn't make the same mistake twice. I checked my phone, but there were no messages. I tried to call her number again, but it was still making that

121

same strange noise. How was I supposed to let her know that I had her case? How were we supposed to sort it out if I couldn't even get hold of her?

It was weird having Lizzie's stuff in my room; almost as if she was with me, but not really. It only made me miss her even more. I still didn't know if she was okay. I couldn't forget the way her dad had dragged her off to the lift when we were saying goodbye—that desperate look she'd given me—and now this. I slipped the necklace back into the case and pulled the lid down. I could tell Nan later, there was no rush. The first thing I needed to do was talk to Bailey.

*   *   *

'Hang on a minute, Bee, start again. This sounds more like an episode of *Sherlock* than a holiday to Spain!'

'Look, I'm not joking, Bailey. I really need your help.' I'd told him everything, right from the moment the first pink envelope arrived.

He got up off his bed and grabbed a notebook and pen from his desk. I stared at him as he crossed the room. I could have sworn he'd grown taller since I'd last seen him. I blushed suddenly, remembering the way Lizzie had teased me about fancying him. It was crazy. How could I fancy Bailey? We were almost like family!

'So let me get this straight,' he said, holding up the pen and notepad like a detective. 'Your mum and dad had been fighting over a letter and then your dad saw the tickets to Spain in the kitchen and disappeared, although he's actually at your Uncle Ron's. And then you met a girl in Spain called

122

Lizzie with an identical suitcase to yours and the day after you met her you noticed your mum had another letter in her bag, in exactly the same sort of envelope as the first one. Then on the last day of the holiday Lizzie told you that her brother died and that she was really scared of her dad. And on the same day, your mum bumped into a woman in the market from her past and totally freaked out and your nan has just told you that the woman was Lizzie's mum. And now you've just discovered that you've brought Lizzie's suitcase home instead of yours. Blimey, Bee!'

'Okay, I know it sounds crazy when you say it like that, but…'

'No, look, I'm taking notes. This is brilliant!' He scribbled something in his notebook. 'So is your dad back from your uncle's yet?'

I shook my head.

'And do you know what was in the first letter?'

I shook my head again. 'Uh-uh.'

'But you're pretty sure it was from Lizzie's mum?'

I nodded. 'It had to be. That's why there was one in Spain too.'

'And you've got Lizzie's suitcase in your room and you think she took yours on purpose so that you'd take hers by mistake.'

'Maybe. I don't know.' It sounded ridiculous, even to me.

'So what I want to know,' said Bailey, still scribbling away in his notebook, 'is have you looked through Lizzie's suitcase to see if she's left you some sort of message or a sign?'

'What do you mean?'

'Honestly, Bee!' He rolled his eyes. 'Have you

123

thought this through at all? Lizzie didn't take your suitcase home because she likes your clothes more than hers, did she? If Lizzie took *your* suitcase home so that you'd take *hers*, she must've done it for a reason. Have you tried calling her?'

'Of course I have, but her phone's dead.'

'What about sending her an email?'

'I can't. My dad took the laptop with him to Uncle Ron's. You know how precious his laptop is, with his project on it and everything!'

Bailey waved at his desk. 'Then use mine.'

I looked at him and then over at the computer. Why hadn't I thought of that? I'd memorized Lizzie's email address as soon as she'd given it to me; it was so easy.

I sat at the computer, nervous suddenly. What if her dad was reading her emails? I didn't want to get her into trouble. In the end, I just wrote that I was worried about her and that she should call me. And then I pressed send.

We both stared at the screen.

'She might not even be at her computer,' I said. 'It might be days before she logs on. She might even—'

There was a *ping* and a new message popped up in Bailey's mailbox.

'Go on then,' he said.

'It's too quick. It's probably not even from her.'

'Just click on it, Bee, come on.'

My hand was shaking. Something was wrong. I could feel it deep inside. Lizzie was in trouble. Bailey nudged me out of the way and clicked on his inbox.

From: Lizzie Munroe
To: Bailey Hunter
Subject: Leave me alone

Don't contact me again. Don't call me or email me. Just forget we ever met each other.
Lizzie

Tears stung my eyes. 'She'd never say that.' I cleared my throat, blinking hard. I didn't want to cry in front of Bailey. 'I only saw her last night and she said, "Promise you won't forget me, whatever happens".'

'What did she mean, *whatever happens*?'

'I don't know. But something's wrong. Her dad must have forced her to write the email, he *must have*, that's the only explanation.'

I turned to Bailey. His face was serious for the first time since I'd arrived. 'We need to check her case,' he said, jumping up and grabbing his phone and keys. 'Come on, let's go straight over to yours and look through it now.'

*   *   *

I'm not exactly sure what Bailey expected to find; a note, or a letter or something. We took each piece of clothing out really carefully, checking in all the pockets. We felt around the lining of the case for hidden messages and shook her books, waiting for something to flutter down to the ground, but there was nothing.

The bottom of the case was covered in her folded beach towel. I lifted it up and gave it a

shake, a scattering of sand falling to the floor.
'Well, that's it,' I said, deflated. 'It's hopeless.'
I dropped the towel back in the case and sank
down onto my bed. 'This is a total nightmare. I'll
probably never see her again in my life.'

'No, wait a minute, what's this?' Bailey fished
something out from the bottom of the case and
handed it to me. It was a small purple notebook
with a purple and silver heart-shaped lock. It
must've been wrapped up in the towel.

'It's her diary,' I whispered. 'Lizzie said she
wrote a diary.'

'Bingo! Read it then, come on. What does it
say?'

'But it's private, Bailey. Look, it's got a lock on it
and everything. What if there's something in there
she doesn't want me to know?'

'*Are you for real, Bee? Don't you see!*' He was
getting frustrated. 'Lizzie took *your* case so you
would take hers and find her diary. It's so obvious.'

'Really?' I said, still unsure.

'Really,' he said firmly.

There was a tiny silver key hanging on a piece of
purple thread. I used it to open the lock and then
turned to the last entry. If Lizzie had been trying to
tell me something when we said goodbye in Spain,
then surely it would be the last thing she'd written.
I stared down at the page. Every line was filled with
Lizzie's messy handwriting, as if she couldn't get
the words out fast enough. But my eyes were drawn
to the four big words right at the bottom.

My heart started to bang in my chest. My breath
was coming too fast, like Mum on the plane.
I blinked and then blinked again as if I could
magic the words away—but they were still there.

126

My breath came faster. I felt dizzy. The room started to spin. Four terrible words that changed everything.

BEE'S DAD KILLED LUKE!

Lizzie

Luke's bedroom had barely changed since he died. The bed was made and it was spotlessly clean, but apart from that, the same posters were up on the walls, the same football trophies proudly displayed on the shelves. It was Luke's room but there was no sense of Luke. It was difficult to believe he'd ever slept in the bed, or hung out listening to music with his mates.

I sat on the edge of the bed, trying to conjure up *something* about my dead brother; some feeling or memory. Mum was always harping on about how much I worshipped him, how I would follow him around like a puppy. She says I used to cry when he went to school. How can I not remember that? And if it's true, how did I cope when he died? How long did I wait for him to come home?

I wanted to know what happened on the night he died, but even more than that, sitting on Luke's bed, in his perfectly preserved bedroom, I wanted to *know* Luke. The holiday had changed everything. It wasn't just meeting Bee. It was finding out that she'd known me before, when I was little; that our families had been close friends. It was like coming full circle—and the circle seemed to start and finish with Luke.

I hated the way Mum talked about Luke as if he'd had a golden halo fixed permanently to his head—the perfect son who could do no wrong. Maybe he had been an angel when he was a little boy, like when he was two or three, but in the last year of his life, Luke had been trouble.

I didn't know all the details, but I knew he'd been kicked out of school. It wasn't Luke's fault of course, as Dad never tired of telling me—it was the school, the lack of discipline, the *other* boys who led him down the wrong path.

And then once, a couple of years ago, we were over at my grandparents and my granddad said something about Luke being a bad penny. He said that just before Luke died he'd been running wild, totally out of control. It caused the most awful row; Mum said Granddad was a bitter old man and that she'd never speak to him again unless he apologized, but Granddad refused. He said it was high time she stopped burying her head in the sand and faced up to the truth.

But what *was* the truth? Was Luke this perfect angel? Or was he totally out of control, like Granddad said? And even if he was, why should that have anything to with Bee's dad? I'd always been told that Luke died in a car accident, but maybe it was Bee's dad who was driving the car? Maybe that was why Dad blamed him? If only I could step back in time—rewind the years to that night in Spain; find out what *really* happened.

The door swung open suddenly, making me jump. It was Mum.

'What on earth are you doing? I heard the bed creaking from downstairs...' Her face was deathly

128

white, as if she'd seen a ghost—or heard one, at any rate.

'I was just sitting here, thinking about Luke.'

Mum's face softened. She walked across the room and sat next to me on the bed, taking my hand. 'Hey, Lizzie, have I ever told you about the time Luke did this sponsored swim? I was listening to the radio just now and there was something on that reminded me.'

I shook my head, although the last thing I wanted was to hear another, 'my perfect son Luke' story.

'He wasn't even the strongest swimmer, to be honest,' Mum went on. 'But this elderly man came up to the school, a veteran, to talk about his experiences in the Second World War. It was part of their history topic. I don't know what he said to them exactly, but Luke came home determined to raise money for the victims of war. He swam 300 lengths over the course of a week and raised £300. We were so proud of him.'

Her face was lit up, as if Luke had the power to reach down from wherever he was and flick a switch on inside her.

'How old was he when he did it?'

'Oh, younger than you are now. Ten, maybe eleven? It was during his last year at primary school.'

Yes, but what about after that? I wanted to say. *What was he like when he was twelve? Thirteen? Fourteen? When he got in with that bad crowd at school? Was he still doing sponsored swims or had he found other ways to fill his time?*

'I did a sponsored silence once, Mum, do you

129

remember? For Children in Need. I didn't speak for a whole day.'

'Sorry, Lizzie, what did you say?'

I shrugged, pulling my hand out of hers. 'Nothing, it doesn't matter.' I could do a sponsored silence for a whole year and she probably wouldn't notice. She was miles away, lost in her memories of Luke. I was so sick of hearing about all his amazing accomplishments. Maybe Granddad was right and Mum was just incapable of facing up to the truth. Facing up to the Luke who was kicked out of school. The Luke who'd been out of control.

Whenever she talked about Luke in that simpering, soppy way, I wanted to stick my fingers in my ears and go 'la la la'. But I envied her in a way. At least she *had* memories. Whenever I tried to remember anything about my big brother, there was just this great gaping hole. It would be easy as anything to fill it up with Mum's memories—to pretend I'd had the perfect brother—but I wanted to know the *real* Luke.

Mum squeezed my hand and stood up. 'I'll just go and try the airport again, see if they've found your suitcase. Your dinner will be ice-cold by now.'

'I'm really not hungry, Mum, sorry.'

I waited until she'd gone back downstairs and then opened the drawer in Luke's old bedside table. I don't know why or what I expected to find—but even so, I found myself looking for clues. Clues about who Luke really was. The drawer was filled with a load of boring stuff. An old tube of superglue, a pack of cards, some grubby elastic bands and, lying at the bottom, a study guide to a Russian novel called *The Death of Ivan Ilyich* by Leo Tolstoy.

I picked the guide up, just to see if there were any notes in there, actual words that Luke had written—I realized suddenly that I didn't even know what his handwriting looked like. I flicked through, but it was clean, not a mark on it; the pages as crisp and fresh as if they'd come straight from the printers. I'd just decided that he'd probably never even touched it, when, right at the end, tucked inside the back cover, I found a photo.

My heart started to beat a bit faster. It was of me and Luke. But it wasn't any old photo. It was a photo of the day Mum had been talking about at the ceremony in Spain: the day Luke put a slice of orange in his mouth to make me laugh. The picture had been taken right there in the same shady, wooded area. There was a blue and white checked picnic blanket and I was sitting in the middle, clapping my hands and squealing in delight, and Luke was on all fours, like a huge, overgrown puppy, grinning at me with his orange-peel smile.

I ran my hand over the photo. It was so vivid. I could almost hear myself shouting, *Orange mouth again, Lukie! Orange mouth again!* Luke looked warm and funny and playful and not out of control at all—and it was as obvious as anything from the expression on my face that he was the most important person in my entire universe.

I'd been surrounded by pictures of Luke for as long as I could remember, but there was something different about this one. This wasn't just a photo of me and Luke. It was a photo of

131

Luke playing with me, making me laugh. The last photo of us together before he disappeared out of my life for ever. I wanted to slip inside the picture. Get to know him again. Find out what he was really like.

I wondered if Mum had seen the photo, if she knew it was stuck in the back of the study guide. I was about to go down and ask her when I noticed there was something written on the back. I turned it over, the words hitting me between the eyes like a hammer. It didn't make sense. Nothing made sense. I read it again, really slowly, trying to take it in.

Hey Luke,
Remember this? Well, anyway, I wanted you to have it.
Sorry for everything.
R.I.P.
Aidan.

Aidan? Aidan was Bee's brother. She'd mentioned him a few times when we were in Spain. She said he'd left home years ago, that she hardly ever saw him. How could he even have had this photo? Was he in the woods with us that day? And what was he apologizing for? And if it really was taken the day before Luke died, *in Spain*, how did it end up here in Luke's bedroom, hidden inside an old study guide?

I lay back on Luke's bed, missing him suddenly, with an awful hollow feeling deep inside. I desperately needed to see Bee, to find out what she knew. Aidan had written R.I.P. on the back of the photo. But how was my big brother supposed to rest in peace when there seemed to be so many unanswered questions surrounding the night he died?

Bee

BEE'S DAD KILLED LUKE!

I held Lizzie's diary up to show Bailey. I was so shocked I just stood there, not saying anything, while he scanned the page.

'What's going on, Bee? Luke is Lizzie's brother, right? Her brother who died! How much do you really know about Lizzie and her family?'

He took the diary out of my hand and started flicking through, reading other entries.

'Did you know about the memorial service in the woods? And there's stuff here about when her mum bumped into your mum at the market.'

'I know about all of that,' I said weakly. 'But...' I tried to get my head round those four awful words. My dad didn't kill Luke. *Lizzie's* dad was the one with the temper. My dad isn't like that. He's quiet and gentle. He likes to blend into the background. Disappear.

'You really need to speak to your dad,' said Bailey. 'Ask him about Lizzie's brother and what happened.'

'But what if Lizzie thinks it's true? What if she actually thinks my dad killed her brother? I bet that's why she sent the email. She thinks my dad killed Luke, so she wants to forget she ever met me. She must hate me so much, that's why she's not

133

texting me back and—'

'Woah, calm down, Bee. I know it *says* that your dad killed Luke, but she was just writing down what her dad told her. That doesn't necessarily mean she thinks it's true.'

I grabbed the diary back and read right through the last page, screwing my eyes up to make sense of her messy handwriting. Maybe Bailey was right. Lizzie sounded just as shocked and upset as me. That was why she'd said, *Promise you won't forget me, whatever happens*, when we'd said goodbye at the hotel. She must've known her dad was going to stop us from seeing each other again.

I sunk down onto my bed. 'What am I going to do, Bailey? How could they say something so awful about my dad? And how am I going to find out what really happened to Luke—what *really* went on between our two families? If only I knew what was in those two letters...'

'Well, that's easy enough, isn't it? Find the letters and read them.'

'Easy? What do you mean, *easy*? I don't know where they are. My dad might have taken the first one with him, for all I know—and I can't get anywhere near my mum to find the second one, not with Nan guarding her!'

'Well then, you'll just have to call your dad.'

'But what if he won't tell me?'

Bailey pulled me up off the bed. 'Blimey, Bee, I never realized you were such a defeatist! He might not tell you. He might pretend he never read it, or that it was an electricity bill or something, but surely it won't hurt to try.'

'I am *not* a defeatist,' I said, getting cross. 'I was going to call him as soon as I got home, but that was before I read the diary. How would you like it if someone accused *your* dad of being a murderer? And anyway, how am I supposed to get Uncle Ron's phone number without my nan or Mum finding out?'

'Well, what about his mobile?'

'I've been calling his mobile for the past two weeks. I've left loads of messages but he doesn't call back. It's hopeless.'

'There you go again,' he said, shaking his head. 'Defeatist! Don't you ever watch any crime shows on TV? I'll distract your nan while you look in her phone for your Uncle Ron's number. Simples!'

'Oh yes, *simples*,' I said sarcastically, but I followed him out of my room and downstairs.

Nan was in the kitchen, stirring a pan of baked beans on the stove.

'Would you like to stop for tea, Bailey?' she said as we came in. 'It's only beans on toast, I'm afraid. That's all I could find in the cupboard.'

'Is Mum eating with us?' I asked, trying to sound as natural as possible.

'She's still upstairs, resting,' said Nan. 'And I'm not going to disturb her. Set the table would you, Bee?'

'Don't worry, I'll do it,' said Bailey, 'and I'd love to stay for tea. How was your holiday, Mrs. Brooks? I heard there was a waiter who had his eye on you. I bet you were fighting them off.'

'Oh, get away with you,' giggled Nan, blushing bright red. 'What's Bee been saying now?'

I grabbed a scrap of paper and a pen and left them talking about Carlos. I'd forgotten how good Bailey was at sweet-talking Nan. He's just got this cheeky way of speaking to her that she loves. When

I go round to his house I can never think of a thing to say to his parents—it's so embarrassing.

Nan's phone was in her handbag by the front door. She only got it about six months ago but I knew all the family phone numbers were in it because I'd helped her add them to her contacts list myself. I felt bad about tricking her in a way, but in another way, I did have the right to speak to my own dad. I unlocked the phone and clicked on contacts. Raymond, Renie, Rita, *Ron*. I copied the number, locked the phone and dropped it back in her bag.

Bailey kept Nan chatting all through tea. I watched him across the table as he entertained her with stories of his camping trip. I'd been so caught up with everything, I hadn't even asked him how it went.

'There was more mud than tent, to be honest,' he was saying. 'My dad kept insisting it was character-building, but even my mum was begging for a hot bath and some clean clothes by the end of the third day, and we only lasted till the fourth.'

'That's a shame,' said Nan. 'We had gorgeous weather, didn't we, Bee? And the pool was lovely. I managed a swim nearly every day.'

'Lucky you,' said Bailey. 'Mind you, it rained so much in Norfolk, we practically had our own private pool right in front of our tent.'

Bailey grinned at me as Nan roared with laughter. I blushed, looking down at my plate, my face burning up. I shook my head. What was wrong with me? I got up to clear the dishes, my stomach in the tightest knot, but only because I was about to call Dad.

We helped Nan to wash up as quickly as we

136

could and raced back upstairs. By the time we got up to my room, the knot in my stomach had turned into a massive great boulder. I hadn't spoken to Dad since the Friday he went missing. That was only three weeks ago, but I was used to seeing him every day and it felt like a lifetime. So much had happened since then; it was almost like calling a stranger.

'I'll keep watch by the door,' said Bailey. 'Just in case your mum gets up, or your nan wants you for something.'

I sat on the edge of the bed, clutching my phone. 'But what am I going to say? I can't just ask him about the letter straight off. I really don't think I can do this, you know.'

'Come on, Bee, just chat to him. Tell him about your holiday. Lull him into a false sense of security and then go in for the kill.'

'*Bailey!*'

'Just *talk* to him, Bee. It's not rocket science.'

I turned to face the wall and dialled the number. It might not be rocket science to Bailey, but what are you supposed to say to your dad when you've just found out that your best friend's parents think he murdered their son? I pressed the numbers really slowly and then held the phone up to my ear. Someone answered straight away. It was Uncle Ron.

'Hello,' I said in a small voice. 'Erm…it's Bee.'

'Oh hello, Bee, my love,' he boomed. 'How are you?'

'I'm fine, thank you, Uncle Ron.' I took a breath. It was difficult to speak. I wanted to hang up. Bailey nodded at me from the door, urging me to keep going.

'Erm, I was just wondering if I could talk to my dad.'

There was a beat. 'Your dad?' said Uncle Ron. 'Your dad's not here.'

'Oh, I'm sorry,' I said. 'Do you think you could ask him to ring me when he gets back?'

'What do you mean, love? What do you mean, when he gets back?'

I clutched the phone even tighter. I could feel my tea churning about in my stomach.

'I haven't spoken to your dad, or seen him, in months.'

Lizzie

I still couldn't take it in. Did this mean Luke and Aidan were friends? My brother and Bee's brother. It was crazy. Aidan must've taken the photo of me and Luke at the picnic. Bee and I were really young back then, just under three, but our brothers were teenagers. They *must* have been mates. Maybe Aidan was even there on the night Luke died—but why was he saying sorry?

I took the photo into my room and slipped it under my pillow. I really needed to talk to Bee, but I felt funny about it at the same time. If only things could go back to the way they were before Dad told me about Bee's dad. It felt as if a hundred years had passed since we were last sitting up on our rock, giggling about the lifeguards and moaning about how hot it was. Now I had questions about her dad *and* her

138

brother and I had a horrible feeling our friendship might never be the same again.

*   *   *

The next morning at breakfast it was business as usual. Or as usual as it could be in our house. Dad was out for a run, but as soon as he got back it would be double maths followed by literacy. No six-week summer holiday for me. It was the same every year, two weeks in Spain and then straight back to lessons.

Mum was at the sink, washing up. 'I still haven't managed to talk to anyone at the airport about your suitcase,' she said as I came in. 'I've left a message but it'll be a miracle if anyone rings back.'

'Hey, Mum, you know that picnic you were telling me about? The one we had just before Luke died?' She turned round, frowning. The toast popped up in the toaster suddenly, making me jump. I took a breath to steady myself. 'You were telling me at the memorial, remember? About how Luke stuck a piece of orange in his mouth to make me laugh.'

'What about it, Lizzie? Why are you bringing it up now?'

I shrugged. 'No reason. I was just thinking about writing a poem.'

'Really?' Mum's face brightened. 'A poem about Luke?'

I nodded. I hadn't planned on saying that at all, it just came out, but it suddenly seemed like the perfect way to pump her for more information. 'I was just wondering if there were any photos of

139

me and Luke together?'

Mum shook her head. 'Not from the picnic. I didn't have my camera with me that day—I left it at the hotel—but I can still remember the whole afternoon as if it happened yesterday.'

'And were we on our own? Or was anyone else there, with us?' I took a bite of toast, trying to breathe normally.

'Were we on our own *where*?' It was Dad, back from his run.

'Nowhere,' I said quickly, hopping up from the table. Why did he always have to creep up on us like that? 'Do you need any help with the dishes, Mum?'

Mum handed me a tea towel but she didn't say anything. I could feel Dad's eyes burning into the back of my head.

'I'm going up to have a shower,' he said. 'I'll be down to start maths in ten minutes.'

Mum waited until she heard the bathroom door close. 'Why did you ask me that, Lizzie? Did Bee say something to you? Did she talk about Luke?'

I looked down at the pan I was drying. 'Of course not. I don't think she even knows that our families knew each other. I wish I could call her, Mum. *Please*. Just to let her know that I'm still her friend. Can't you give me her home phone number? I'm begging you.'

'I can't,' said Mum, automatically looking towards the door. 'Your dad's forbidden you to ever have contact with her again. I'm not saying I agree with him, but I have to respect his wishes.'

'But what about *my* wishes? When are you going to respect my wishes?' I bashed the pan down on the side. 'Bee's my best friend. I can't

140

help it if her family were involved in Luke's death, especially as no one will tell me what really happened.'

Mum took a step towards me. 'Stop shouting!' she hissed nervously, her eyes darting to the door again. If only she wasn't so scared. 'Luke died in an accident. Your father insists that Bee's dad was to blame, but it was an accident, Lizzie. Just a terrible, tragic accident.'

'I know, Mum, you keep telling me. But what about Bee's brother, Aidan? Was he in Spain? Was he at the picnic?'

Mum's hands flew up to her face. 'No he wasn't. No one was at the picnic. Why do you keep asking me that?'

A door slammed and we heard Dad coming down the stairs.

'It's for my poem,' I lied. 'I just want to know about Luke—about his friends and his last days in Spain. That's all.'

I left her in the kitchen and ran upstairs to get my maths book. How did Aidan get that photo if he wasn't at the picnic? Or was Mum lying? She'd definitely looked shocked when I mentioned Aidan's name.

The next two hours were like torture. I thought I was going to die of boredom. Fractions and decimals and negative numbers. I just didn't get how Dad could act as if nothing had happened after dropping such a huge bombshell on me. I didn't want to know about converting fractions to decimals, I wanted to know about Aidan and Luke and Bee's dad and what really happened ten years ago in Spain.

'Mum says you're writing a poem about Luke,'

141

Dad said suddenly, almost as if he could read my mind. 'We can use your literacy lesson to work on it if you want. We haven't done a poetry unit for ages.'

I was about to say no, that anything I wrote about Luke would be private and I wasn't planning on writing a stupid poem anyway— Bee was the one who was good at poetry—but I clamped my mouth shut. If Dad thought I was writing about Luke, if I could get him talking about the past, he might let his guard slip and reveal something about the night Luke died.

'Okay,' I said, as casually as I could. 'We'll do it in literacy.'

I lowered my head, pretending to finish my maths, but it was impossible to concentrate. I owed it to Bee to find out what really happened— for the sake of our friendship. But even more than that, more than anything in the world, I owed it to my big brother Luke.

Bee

I don't know what I said to Uncle Ron after that, I think I just hung up. *He hadn't seen my dad or spoken to him in months.* Mum was lying. She took that call when the policeman was round. She said he was staying at Uncle Ron's and that he was fine, but it wasn't true. He must have called her from somewhere else, but why would she lie about something like that?

'What did he say?' asked Bailey. 'What's the matter?'

'He's not there.' I was still gripping the phone in my hand, a million thoughts piling up in my head. 'My dad's not there. Uncle Ron hasn't seen him in months.'

'Where is he then?'

My eyes met Bailey's. I wished I knew the answer to that. But there was no way of knowing where he was. He could be anywhere.

'What if the first letter was from Lizzie's dad, threatening him or something? He might be on the run, like a real criminal. I mean, think about it. The letter arrives, it causes the most almighty row and then, a few days later, Dad disappears. He's in trouble, Bailey, he must be. That's why my mum lied to the police. She didn't want them to start searching for him.'

'Calm down, Bee. Didn't you say the letter was addressed to your mum?'

'I *know*, but maybe he sent it to my mum to tell her he was coming after my dad. Seriously, Bailey, what other explanation is there?' I could feel myself getting hysterical. Where was my dad? What if he was scared or hurt? What if Lizzie's dad was hunting him down?

'What about your brother?'

'*My brother?* What's he got to do with any of this?'

'Well, think about it, Bee. You were *all* on holiday in Spain ten years ago, weren't you? So if you can't talk to your dad about the night of the accident, and your mum and nan are hiding stuff from you, why don't you ask Aidan?'

I opened my mouth and closed it again. I wanted to fling my arms round Bailey and kiss him.

'Oh my God, you're a genius! Why didn't I think

143

of that?' I jumped up and then froze as my hopes came crashing back down. 'But I don't know where he is. He moved just after Christmas and I don't know his new address. He hasn't been round for ages and you know how private Aidan is. He never tells me anything.'

'Well, you could ask your mum or your nan, couldn't you? They must know where he's living.'

'I'm not sure they know where he is either. My dad and Aidan had this massive fight last Christmas. Aidan was winding Dad up all through lunch. It was like someone picking at a scab over and over until it bleeds. He's only been round once since then to pick up some of his stuff when he moved, but it's not as if they made up or anything...' I trailed off, remembering how awful it was.

Bailey stood there for a moment, thinking, and then grabbed my arm. 'Come on, I've got an idea. We need to go back to mine.'

'Why, what are we going to do?'

He pulled me out of my room and down the stairs. 'We're going to find him online.'

*　　　*　　　*

There were only four Aidan Brooks on Facebook and none of them had a photo of themselves as their profile picture. Bailey sent them all a friend request with a simple message explaining who he was. Just, *Hi, it's your old neighbour Bailey from Westbourne Drive. Bee needs to get in touch with you. You can contact her through my Facebook page. Bailey.*

'What do we do now?'

'Wait, I suppose. It might be days before we hear anything.'

I lay back on Bailey's bed. 'I can't believe that two weeks ago my biggest concern was Melissa Knight and her stupid mates, and now my dad's missing, he's been accused of murdering Lizzie's brother, and I have no way of *seeing* Lizzie, or talking to her or even finding out if she's okay.'

'Who's Melissa Knight?' said Bailey, turning round from his desk.

My face grew hot. I sat up, realizing I'd never told him. 'Oh, just some girl who's been on my case at school. It's no big deal.'

He rolled his eyes. 'Now who's lying? Why didn't you tell me before?'

'I don't tell you everything, you know. I didn't want to go on about it. Can we just drop it, Bailey, please?'

'Okay, okay, consider it dropped,' he said, holding his hands up. 'So what school does Lizzie go to?'

'She doesn't go to school. Her dad teaches her at home.'

'You're kidding me!'

'I'm not, it's true. She says it's grim. She's *never* been to school. When she was really young, her mum used to teach her with these two boys who live at the end of her street, Danesh and Dilan, but then when she was...'

I stopped mid-sentence.

'What is it? What's the matter?'

'I've just remembered something,' I said. 'It's about Dilan. When I told Lizzie about Melissa Knight and Glendale High—'

'Oh, so you told *Lizzie* about Melissa Knight,'

145

said Bailey, interrupting me, pretending to look hurt.

'*Bailey!* Stop being such a baby! This is important... When I *told* Lizzie, she said she knew Glendale High because it was right near to where she lived, and then this other time she was telling me about how much she likes Dilan and how he lives at the end of her street and that he's always in the garden, messing about with his bike.'

'So what are you suggesting?' said Bailey sarcastically. 'That we go and look at all the roads near your school until we find a house with a boy fixing his bike in the garden. Talk about looking for a needle in a haystack!'

'No, that's not all,' I said, excited now for the first time. 'She said she calls him *C.C.* which stands for *Cromwell Corner* because he lives in the corner house of her street. It was like a code or something, just in case her dad ever read her diary. I didn't think anything of it at the time but her street must be called Cromwell Road or Cromwell Avenue, and we know it's near my school...'

'Okay, fine,' said Bailey, turning back to the computer. 'So let's say we find out where this boy Dilan lives. How's that going to help exactly?'

'*Blimey, Bailey!* I thought you were the one with all the ideas. If we find Dilan, we can go round there and give him a note to give to Lizzie explaining exactly what's going on—and then she can give him a note to give back to me. Her parents already know him so he'll be the perfect go-between. Simples!'

*   *   *

146

Finding Lizzie's street turned out to be really easy. The clues led us straight there. Bailey had printed out a map of the area around Glendale High on the computer and we found a Cromwell Road and a Cromwell Close both within easy walking distance. I wanted to catch the bus and look for the house right away, but Bailey was off to visit his grandparents for the weekend so we arranged to meet up first thing Monday morning.

Mum was up and about and busy again by the time I got home, unpacking and organizing the house. I was dying to tell her that I'd spoken to Uncle Ron and that I knew Dad wasn't really staying there, but I had this horrible feeling that if I confronted her she might say something about Dad and the death of Lizzie's brother. Something I really didn't want to hear. I just wished I knew where he was. It was bad enough when I'd thought he was staying at Uncle Ron's, but knowing now that he could be literally *anywhere* was a hundred times worse.

I started to wonder about Aidan too. Why he never came round any more and why he'd always had such a terrible relationship with Dad. One of my earliest memories is of Aidan yelling at Dad across the kitchen table, while I sat with my hands pressed over my ears. I just remember Aidan being angry *all* the time, while Dad refused to rise to the bait. Was it because Aidan knew something about Dad and Lizzie's brother? Is that what all their rows were about?

He is twenty-four now and I hardly ever see him. Nan had moved into his bedroom after my granddad Harry died. It was supposed to have been for a few weeks, until she got used to being on her own, but it had been more than a year now and she was still with us. Bit by bit, over the months, I'd helped Mum to box up some stuff Aidan still had at home, and he'd finally come over to shift it just after that awful row with Dad at Christmas.

That was the last time he'd been round. Eight months ago. Mum had begged him to come for a meal on her birthday but he'd said he had other plans. It was a miserable day. Mum moped about for hours, hoping he'd change his mind and show up to surprise her, and then ended up getting furious with Dad, saying it was his fault that Aidan didn't want to be with his family, and that he was the only one who could put things right.

I didn't pay much attention at the time—it was only now, looking back, that I started to wonder what Mum meant, and if it had anything to do with the holiday in Spain ten years ago. Aidan would've been fourteen the year Luke died. Old enough to remember what really happened. Did he know something about Dad? Is that what Mum meant when she said only Dad could put things right?

I thought Monday would never come. I had no idea if Aidan had contacted Bailey on Facebook, or if he was even *on* Facebook, or if we'd ever find Dilan's house and get a message to Lizzie. The plan seemed less and less likely to work as the hours crawled by. For all we knew, Dilan could be away for the whole summer—or even if we did manage to find the right house, and he was there, he might refuse to take the message to Lizzie.

I came very close to texting Bailey at his grandparents' to tell him to forget the whole idea, but I didn't want him to think I was wimping out, or being 'defeatist', as he put it. He was so convinced we'd hear something back from Aidan, I had to go along with it, however far-fetched it seemed.

I kept the note to Lizzie really short, just writing that I'd read her diary and was trying to contact my brother to find out the truth. I also asked whether she believed what her dad had said about my dad. I was terrified she'd say she did, but I had to know.

I was up and out of the house by nine on Monday morning. Mum had left for work and Nan was still in bed, so it was easy to get away. I was praying Bailey would be ready to go, but he was still eating his breakfast.

'We didn't get back until really late,' he said, gulping down the rest of his cereal. 'The traffic was terrible and then we had to stop about three times so my mum could go to the loo, and—'

'It's alright, I don't need all the details,' I said, interrupting him. 'Just hurry up, can't you? Dilan might go out for the day if we don't get there soon.'

'Okay, calm down. I'm coming. Have you written the message?'

I nodded, hopping from foot to foot, impatient to get going. 'Yes, it's in my bag. Come on, let's go.'

The bus came straight away. It was the 243, the same bus I caught every morning to go to school. A familiar feeling of dread settled over me. My stomach was in knots. So much rested on us finding Dilan and getting the message to Lizzie. I really needed to know that she was okay and that she didn't believe that Dad had anything to do with Luke's death.

We got off right near Glendale High and followed Bailey's map until we came to Cromwell Road. It was a really long street and I could see straight away that none of the houses had front

149

gardens. I stopped to look at the map again. 'Lizzie said Dilan was always out front, in the garden, messing about with his bike, so it can't be this one. Let's try Cromwell Close.'

Cromwell Close was just off Cromwell Road. It was a quiet no-through road with about twenty houses. The houses were much bigger than in Cromwell Road and they all had massive front gardens with gravel paths and fancy-shaped bushes. Our house could have easily fitted inside any one of these houses two or three times over!

'This must be it,' I whispered, as if Dilan, or even worse, Lizzie's dad, might appear at any moment. 'Let's start at the bottom and walk up, checking each garden as we go.'

It felt really weird walking up the road, not knowing if Lizzie might be home—or if she might even be watching us through her bedroom window. We peered into every garden; all of them neat and tidy with carefully mowed lawns—so perfect, it was impossible to tell them apart. I didn't care how defeatist I sounded—the whole plan was ridiculous.

'This is hopeless. We're never going to find it, not in a million years.'

'Hang on a minute,' said Bailey, pointing at the first house on the other side of the close. 'That's on the corner, right? And look in the garden...'

The house on the corner had a massive front garden like all the others. And in the garden there was a dismantled bike, the handlebars lying on the ground next to one of the wheels. I didn't know how we'd missed it first time round. I grabbed Bailey's arm, my heart banging in my chest. 'You go and knock on the door,' I hissed. 'I'm too scared.'

'Don't be stupid. Lizzie's your friend. You need to do it.'

I shook my head, pulling the note out of my pocket. It was in an envelope, with Lizzie's name written across the front. 'Please, Bailey. What if his dad answers? What if he wants to know how I know Dilan? I'll mess it up, I know I will. It's my one chance to make contact with Lizzie and I'll mess it up.'

'Holy Maloney, Bee, get a grip! You're not going to mess it up. Just because Lizzie's dad's a bit psycho, it doesn't mean Dilan's dad will be too.' He pushed me towards the house. 'Go on, you can do it.'

He was right. I had to pull myself together, for Lizzie's sake; for the sake of our friendship. It didn't matter what Dilan's dad was like. I was just a girl, knocking on the door with a message for Lizzie. It was no big deal. There was no time to freak out. I had to be strong. I pushed back my shoulders, took a deep breath and walked up the path.

A boy opened the door. He was seriously cute; very tall, with spiky black hair and a small gold stud in his left ear. I had no idea if he was Dilan or his younger brother, Danesh.

'Dilan?' I said, taking a chance, my fingers crossed behind my back. He looked me up and down, nodding.

'Erm, you don't know me, but I'm a friend of Lizzie Munroe. My name's Bee.'

He didn't say anything for a moment. It was really awkward. I was certain he was going to shut the door in my face, or say 'Lizzie *who?*' but after what seemed like an age he smiled and said, 'Hi,

151

Bee. What's up?'

He listened really carefully as I explained the whole story—well, not the whole story, just that I'd met Lizzie in Spain, and I needed to speak to her but her dad had forbidden us to have any contact with each other. He asked loads of questions, like what was in the note and how could I be so sure she wanted to see me again. I told him as much as I could without mentioning Luke or my dad and what was really going on.

'She lives at number 12,' he said in the end, 'just a few houses up on the left. Why don't you just put the note through the door yourself? I haven't spoken to Lizzie for years.'

'Because I won't know if she gets it—what if her dad reads it first? And because I was wondering if you might be able to bring a note back from her so that I know she's okay. The last time I saw her, the night before we left Spain, she was really scared.'

He looked over my head at Bailey. I wouldn't have blamed him for a second if he thought it was some sort of massive wind-up.

'She told me all about you,' I added in desperation. 'About how you guys used to have lessons together with her mum and how much fun it was…' I trailed off, trying to remember what else she'd said, apart from the fact that she really liked him.

'Okay then, I'll do it.'

My head snapped up. *'Really?'*

Dilan nodded. 'Give me the note and wait for me here, in the garden. I'll go up there now. I don't know if I'll get past her dad, he's really strict, but I'll do my best.'

Lizzie

I was lying on Luke's bed, staring at the photo of us that day at the picnic. I'd started to spend most of my spare time in his room, mainly because it was the best place to hide away from Dad. Sometimes I just lay there thinking about everything that had happened, but sometimes I found myself chatting to him. I didn't expect him to answer or anything, I just liked to tell him stuff—like how much I was missing Bee and how awful things were at home.

I used to blame Luke for everything. I thought it was his fault that Dad was such a nightmare and that Mum was so sad all the time, and that I had to be homeschooled. I was convinced he'd ruined everything. I wanted Mum and Dad to forget about him; to stop missing him so much, to remember they had a daughter who deserved a normal life. I know it sounds awful but I *hated* having a dead brother.

But something had changed. Lying on his bed, staring at the photo of him with his orange-peel mouth, I started to miss Luke for the first time. I remember my grandma saying once that I was just like him; she said I had his spirit. I didn't take much notice back then, it was just another boring conversation about Luke, but I couldn't stop thinking about it now. Maybe he was a bit wild and maybe he did get into trouble at school, but that didn't mean he was a bad person.

Dad's temper had been worse than ever since we got back from Spain—the slightest thing could set him off. I desperately wanted to ask him about Aidan and Luke and whether they'd been friends, but I knew I'd have to pick my moment very carefully if I was going to get him to reveal anything about Luke and the past.

I'd tried talking to him while we were working on my poem in literacy. I asked him if Luke and Bee's brother, Aidan, used to hang out together. He'd looked up from the book he was flicking through, his eyes like lasers. 'Write about Luke if you want,' he said, 'but leave the Brooks family out of it.' His eyes stayed fixed on my face.

'But were they friends?' I persisted, doing my best to keep my voice steady. I was shaking inside but I forced myself to carry on. 'Were they even the same age?'

'I mean it, Lizzie.' He leaned so far forward his face was practically touching mine. 'Don't mention them again, *ever*. Is that clear?'

'Not really,' I muttered under my breath, but I didn't dare ask again.

He was just as angry with Mum. I could hear them arguing now. They were in the kitchen, so I could only catch snatches of what they were saying, but it was something to do with Bee's mum again. I crept out of Luke's room and crouched at the top of the stairs. Dad was shouting, his words bouncing off the walls like bullets.

'It wasn't just a coincidence that she was there at the same time as us, was it? You pretended to be so shocked that you bumped into her at the market, but you knew all along!'

I couldn't hear if Mum said anything back—she was probably crying anyway—but I could hear

154

Dad as loud and clear as if he was standing right in front of me.

'*How could you be so stupid?*' he yelled. '*Why did you go behind my back? What good did you think would come of it?*'

I shrank back against the wall, as if he was shouting at me, but then there was a crash and I knew I had to do something. I raced down the stairs and burst into the kitchen. Someone had to protect Mum from Dad's temper. They both spun round to look at me. Mum was by the sink, a broken plate on the floor, and Dad was on the other side of the room, his arms up in the air, as if he'd been waving them about.

'Go to your room, Lizzie,' he said, his voice low and menacing.

'No, I don't want to.' I stood there with my arms folded, pretending I wasn't scared, even though my heart was racing a million miles a minute.

He took a step towards me. 'Now, Lizzie. Don't make me say it again.'

'Go on, Lizzie,' said Mum. 'We were just talking. Everything's fine.' She was wringing her hands, her eyes brimming with tears.

I shook my head, looking back at Dad—standing up to him for the first time in my life. 'I'm sorry, but I'm not going to my room. I want to know what's going on. I want to know what you were talking about—how Mum went behind your back. I've got a right to know.'

I thought Dad was going to explode. '*GET UP TO YOUR ROOM!*' he roared, taking another step towards me. But I shook my head again, trying not to cry. My feet were rooted to the kitchen floor. 'It doesn't matter how much you shout and get angry and bully us,' I said, my voice rising. 'It won't bring Luke back.'

There was a sudden, terrible silence. Mum rushed over, standing between me and Dad as if she was scared he was going to hit me, but Dad had gone limp, his face crumpled up like an old tissue.

'Just go, Lizzie!' cried Mum. 'Go on, do what your father says.'

I shifted to the side so I could lock eyes with Dad. I didn't know what to do. I didn't know whether to go or stand my ground. I didn't want to make things worse for Mum but I was so sick of the way Dad's moods dominated everything. My brain felt scrambled up—I couldn't think straight, or move or speak or anything. There was so much I wanted to say but I was paralysed.

And then, out of the blue, the doorbell rang; loud and shrill in the silence.

'I'll get it!' I cried, lurching forward, the awful spell broken.

'Just leave it!' warned Dad.

But it was too late. I slipped out of the kitchen and down the hall towards the front door. Dad couldn't carry on shouting at me if someone else was here, even if it was only the postman or the man who comes to read the meter. Mum and Dad bolted after me. Dad pushed past Mum and reached for my arm, but he wasn't quick enough. I got to the door first and pulled it open.

The three of us stood there, staring at the boy on the doorstep. My heart started to race even faster. It wasn't the postman *or* the meter man. It was Dilan.

Time seemed to stand still. I know people

are always saying that, but it's true—it can really happen. Dilan stood on the doorstep and I stood in front of him and Mum and Dad stood behind me and it was as if we'd all forgotten how to speak or move or even blink. I wondered if he'd heard Dad shouting—if that was why he'd knocked on the door. I tried to think of something to say, *anything*, but my mind was completely blank.

It was Mum who recovered first. She slipped past Dad and pulled me to one side so she could greet Dilan properly.

'What a lovely surprise,' she said. 'How are you, Dilan? How are your mum and dad?'

Dilan smiled. 'Fine, thank you, Mrs. Munroe. We're all fine.' He looked nervous, frightened even. Not the confident, cheeky boy I remembered from our lessons.

'I'm going up to my study,' said Dad, turning away. 'And I don't want to be disturbed. I'll be down in half an hour for maths, okay, Lizzie?'

I glanced back at him, nodding.

'Don't worry, we'll be as quiet as we can,' said Mum, as Dad went up. 'Come in, Dilan. Would you like a drink?'

'Just some water, if that's okay,' said Dilan. He was staring at me; his eyes fixed on mine as he stepped into the house, closing the door behind him. My face started to burn up. What was he doing here? Why was he coming in? He hadn't spoken a word to me for the past five years and now suddenly he was standing in my house.

Mum went back to the kitchen. I wanted to say something but my mouth was too dry. We were strangers. I'd been dreaming about him for

157

months and months, desperate to talk to him, but so much time had passed since we'd had our lessons together, it was as if we'd never met before.

'We've just got back from Spain,' I said in the end. I don't know why, but it was better than standing there in silence.

'I know,' he said.

'What do you mean?'

He opened his mouth to speak but Mum popped her head round the kitchen door. 'Come on, you two. How about a slice of cake or a biscuit?'

The second she turned back into the kitchen, Dilan pulled me towards him. 'Listen, Lizzie, I've just met your friend Bee.'

'*Bee?*' My chest was tight suddenly, as if my lungs had stopped working.

'Look, she's written this note to you.' He reached into his pocket and pulled out an envelope. 'She wants you to read it and write back to her, now, while I'm here. I'll sit with your mum for a bit, but hurry up.' He thrust the envelope at me and walked into the kitchen.

I tried to take a proper breath. Dilan knew Bee. He had a message from her. He'd seen her. It didn't make sense. None of it made sense. Mum popped her head round again.

'Come on, Lizzie, don't leave Dilan sitting in here on his own.'

'I'm just going to the loo, Mum. I'll be down in a sec.'

I raced upstairs and locked myself in the bathroom. The message was short and to the point. I recognized her writing from her book of poems. It was small and neat and urgent.

Lizzie, I've read your diary, it was a brilliant idea to swap the cases. My dad's not staying at my Uncle Ron's. I don't actually know where he is but I'm trying to get hold of Aidan to see if he knows anything. Bailey's helping me. Write back that you're okay and that you don't believe your dad. My dad could never hurt anyone. I swear to you, Lizzie, it wasn't him. He didn't kill Luke. We need to find out the truth. See what you can find out from your parents. I keep wishing we were back at the *Globo Rojo*, or sitting up on our rock. Miss you loads…
Bee xxxxxx

I still didn't get it. How did she know Dilan? And how did she get him to bring the note round? And why was her dad hiding away somewhere if he was innocent? I had so many questions but there wasn't time. I crept out of the bathroom and into my room, grabbing a pen off my desk.

I'm fine, I scribbled on the other side of the note. *Maybe we could meet at Dilan's house to talk later this week? If you've heard from Aidan by then we could go and see him together. I think Luke and Aidan were friends. I've found something. I'll tell you when I see you, miss you too, Lizzie xxx*

I stuffed it in the envelope and ran back downstairs.

'Oh, there you are,' said Mum as I came into the kitchen. She was slicing up a lemon sponge

159

cake. 'We were beginning to wonder what happened to you. I was just telling Dilan about the holiday and the mix up with the suitcases. Someone from the airport was supposed to be calling me this morning, but I haven't heard a word!' She was nervous, I could tell. She was probably worried that Dilan had heard Dad shouting at me.

'I don't want any cake, thanks, but Dad said could he have a cup of tea?'

'Are you sure? I thought he said he didn't want to be disturbed.'

'I know, but he called to me just now when I was in the loo.'

I was desperate for her to leave the kitchen so I could talk to Dilan properly. She switched the kettle on, glancing up nervously, as if Dad was watching her.

'My brother made us all tea the other day,' said Dilan suddenly, 'but he forgot to boil the kettle. It was so funny.'

Mum smiled, relaxing a bit. 'He was probably just trying to be helpful. I think Lizzie did that once, didn't you?'

I nodded, my eyes fixed on the kettle. It seemed to be taking an age to boil. How could it take so long? It was like torture waiting for the switch to click off.

'Listen, I've written a note back to Bee,' I said to Dilan, the second Mum shuffled out of the kitchen with a cup of tea for Dad. 'But I need to see her. I know this sounds crazy, but is there any way I could meet her round at yours?'

'But why aren't you allowed to see her? Why can't she come here?'

160

'I can't tell you,' I said. 'It's too complicated. You probably wouldn't believe me anyway. But *please*, Dilan. Can I tell my mum that you've asked me round or something?'

He stared at me for a moment, frowning. 'But she's outside my house right this minute,' he said. 'Why don't you just walk down there with me now?'

'I can't, I've got maths, and anyway my dad wouldn't let me. But he always goes to his office on a Wednesday morning for a meeting. He never misses it.' I could hear Mum on the stairs.

'Maths?' said Dilan. 'In the holidays? Don't you get a break or anything?'

I felt like shaking him. He was asking too many questions. 'Look, I don't get a break. It's not like normal school. *Please, Dilan. I'm begging you.*'

'Okay,' he said. 'I'll say you're invited for lunch on Wednesday. But only if you promise to tell me what's going on when you come round. Deal?'

'Deal,' I said. I would've said anything at that point. 'Here's the note.'

'Dad didn't want tea,' said Mum, coming into the kitchen.

'Really? I was sure I heard him call.'

Dilan stood up, slipping the envelope into his pocket.

'Are you off already, Dilan? You've only just got here.'

'He just came round to invite me over for lunch,' I said. 'The day after tomorrow at twelve, right, Dilan?'

'Oh, how lovely,' said Mum. 'Thank you very much.'

'That's okay,' said Dilan. 'And thanks for the

161

drink.'

I walked him to the door.

'I'll never forget this, Dilan, seriously. And the lunch is just a cover, right? You don't really have to cook for me or anything.'

'I wasn't going to,' he said, looking uncomfortable. 'See you on Wednesday.'

Bee

I watched Dilan as he walked back from Lizzie's house. His hands were in his pockets, his shoulders hunched up around his ears. I couldn't believe it when he handed me the envelope—I just couldn't believe the plan had worked. I felt like dancing in the street.

'What happened? Was her dad there? Is she okay? What did she say?' I was so desperate for news I wanted to shake the answers out of him.

'It was pretty bad actually,' said Dilan, leaning against the wall outside his house. 'Her dad was there, they were arguing just before I rang on the doorbell. I could hear them through the door.'

'What were they saying? Was it about my dad?'

'I don't know, he was just shouting at her to get up to her room, but then when she answered the door to me, they all acted like nothing was wrong. Why would they be arguing about your dad? Is that why you're not allowed to see each other?'

I glanced at Bailey; I wasn't sure how much to say.

'It's a big mess,' said Bailey. 'Stuff that happened years ago.'

Dilan nodded as if he understood. 'Well anyway, she wants to meet you here on Wednesday, at twelve o'clock.'

'Really? This Wednesday? That's amazing!' I was still clutching hold of the note. I folded it in half and slipped it into my bag.

'Aren't you going to open it?' said Dilan. He looked a bit disappointed but I didn't want to read it in front of him or Bailey, just in case there was something bad in it.

'I'll open it at home, but I'll definitely come on Wednesday. Are you sure you don't mind?' He was so nice. No wonder Lizzie liked him so much.

'No, it's fine,' he said, shrugging. 'It's the holidays so there's nothing going on anyway.' He turned to go back into his house. 'See you then.'

'Thanks again,' I said.

'Yeah, cheers,' said Bailey. 'See you around.'

*   *   *

I waited until I was back at home and on my own before I read Lizzie's note. I held my breath as I pulled it out of the envelope, praying she'd say she didn't believe her dad, but she hadn't even mentioned it. It was really short, just a couple of lines—something about Aidan and Luke being friends. I hadn't even thought of Aidan until Bailey mentioned him yesterday, but it seemed so obvious now. Luke and Aidan had probably been friends for years before Lizzie and I were even born.

It was so weird to think of our families knowing each other when Lizzie and I were babies. Our mums must've been really close to go on holiday together, but I still didn't know how they'd met in the first place. Lizzie's road was seriously posh compared with ours—they obviously had loads more money than us—but maybe they'd met through work or something like that?

Mum was in a much better mood when she came home from work. She's in charge of the X-ray department at our local hospital and she loves it. It's very chaotic and she's always run off her feet, but she says she'd much rather be busy than sitting around all day with nothing to do. Sometimes I think she'd like to be in charge of the whole hospital!

'Nan's out shopping,' I said, pouring her a cup of tea. 'She said not to cook anything for dinner; she'll do it when she gets back.'

Mum kicked her shoes off and sank down onto the couch. 'God, that's a relief.' She leaned over to rub her feet. 'It was crazy today. It's always like that when I've been away. It takes me at least two weeks to get the office back the way I like it. Dr. Mason said the whole place would go to pot if it wasn't for me.'

'Is that where you met Lizzie's mum?' I asked, sitting down next to her. 'At the hospital?'

Mum shook her head, frowning. 'I told you all about that, on the way back from Spain.'

'No, you just said you were really close, you didn't say where you actually met.'

She leaned back, sighing heavily. 'I met her when I was pregnant with you, Bee. We got chatting at the clinic one day while we were both waiting for a scan. It was during the school holidays so I had Aidan with me—he was pretty excited to see a picture of his new baby sister—and Suzie was there with Luke...' She closed her eyes, as if it was painful to remember.

'Are you okay?' I really wanted her to carry on talking but I was worried she might start hyperventilating again like she did on the plane.

'I'm fine, Bee, it's just so sad when I think of how happy we were back then. Anyway we were at the clinic, chatting, and we realized that we both had a big gap between our first babies and our second. Aidan was eleven then and Luke had just turned twelve. It gave us lots to talk about. We were very different in lots of ways, but we just clicked, if you know what I mean.'

I knew exactly what she meant; it was just like me and Lizzie.

'We swapped numbers and then after you and Lizzie, or Elizabeth as she was called back then, were born, we began to hang out together. It was so easy. The two boys would play football in the garden, and we would sit drinking endless cups of coffee, nattering on about our beautiful new babies.'

'So she was your best friend?'

'Yes, I suppose she was,' said Mum. 'Dad really liked her as well, although I think he always found Lizzie's dad Michael quite difficult to take. He was much more dominant than Dad, throwing his weight about, dictating what we did when we went out, that sort of thing. I used to wonder how she put up with it, to be honest.'

I knew all about Lizzie's dad throwing his weight around but I didn't say anything. 'How about Aidan and Luke—did they get on?'

'They did to start off with; they went to the same school and even though they were in different years, outside school they were inseparable. But

165

during that last year, leading up to the accident, Luke changed a lot.'

'What do you mean?'

Mum frowned. 'I don't like to talk about it really, it feels disloyal to Suzie… It's just that he seemed older suddenly, much older than Aidan. He'd started drinking and getting into all sorts of trouble. It was driving Suzie to despair. Things got worse and worse until finally, just before we were due to go to Spain, he was permanently excluded from school.'

'And what about him and Aidan? Did they stay friends?'

'They did, but it wasn't good. Luke started to push Aidan around, put him down, make out he wasn't old enough to be his friend. Aidan was still too young to understand why the friendship had changed. He was a year younger than Luke, don't forget, and he worshipped him. He would've walked on hot coals if Luke had asked him to.'

So Mum and Suzie were best friends, and then Aidan and Luke, and now me and Lizzie. It was as if we were destined to be friends, destined to meet in Spain. I couldn't wait to see her on Wednesday, but there was something about her note that had been bothering me—niggling away at the back of my mind—and every time I thought of it, a sour feeling like acid filled my stomach.

It was about my dad. I'd asked Lizzie to write back that she didn't believe he was responsible for Luke's death—but she hadn't mentioned it. She hadn't said anything about Dad at all, just that she'd found something, and that she wanted to visit Aidan with me. I turned back to Mum, wondering if she'd open up to me, tell me what

166

really happened.

'Do you know anything about Luke's accident?' I asked, scared of what she might say, but desperate to know at the same time. 'Do you know what happened the night he died?'

Her cheeks flushed and she looked away, as if she was trying to decide what to say, but just at that moment Nan arrived back.

'Any chance of a hand with these bags?' she called out from the front door, and Mum jumped up from the couch to help her.

I'd just have to wait until I saw Lizzie—until she told me what she'd found. The acid burned its way round my body. What if it was something that linked my dad to Luke's death? What if she'd found something that proved beyond doubt that he was guilty?

Lizzie

It was lessons as usual when Dad came down from the study. Converting fractions into decimals. I found it impossible to concentrate. I couldn't believe Bee was down the road at Dilan's and that I was going to see her on Wednesday. I kept going over what she'd said in her note, that her dad wasn't staying at her Uncle Ron's and that she didn't know where he was. Why would he disappear like that if he had nothing to hide?

Bee's dad was missing, but Aidan had written *Sorry for everything* on the back of the photo. Was he saying sorry for something that happened before the night of the accident? Or did he do something to *cause* the accident? I had to talk to him. I had to ask him why he was apologizing and how the orange-peel photo ended up in Luke's bedside drawer. I was desperate to find out more about Luke and Aidan and their friendship before I saw Bee on Wednesday.

I looked across the table at Dad—he was setting me more sums. An hour ago he'd been yelling at me to get upstairs and I'd stood up to him for the first time in my life—and now he was sitting there, churning out work for me like a machine. He was an expert at turning fractions into decimals but he couldn't even talk to his own daughter. There had to be some way to get through to him; some way to find out what really happened to Luke in Spain.

'Can I work on my poem instead of maths?' I said when he handed me the next sheet. 'I'm finding it so difficult to concentrate at the moment.'

He glanced up, shaking his head slightly, almost as if he was surprised to see me sitting there. 'Fractions first, Lizzie. We've got a timetable to stick to.'

'But can't we change the timetable?' I said, feeling a tiny bit bolder. 'Just for today? What was Luke's favourite subject?' I went on quickly. 'Was he good at maths? Or did he prefer science, or ICT?'

Dad sat back in his chair, looking at me properly for the first time in what felt like years.

'Luke was good at most subjects,' he said, 'but he didn't apply himself. It was all too easy for him.'

168

'He probably got bored,' I said. 'I bet that's why he got into trouble with those other boys at school.'

'Sending him to that school was the biggest mistake we ever made,' said Dad. He looked away, his face filled with pain. I felt bad suddenly. It was difficult for me to remember anything specific about Luke, but Dad probably had a million painful memories.

'Do you still miss him?' I said. 'Is that why you're so angry all the time?'

Dad turned back towards me. His eyes were glistening, as if the ice had started to melt. 'I can't talk about it, Lizzie,' he said. 'He's gone and there's nothing we can do about it. That's what your mother doesn't understand, with her ceremonies and anniversaries. You were right when you said shouting and yelling won't bring Luke back. Nothing will bring him back and that's all there is to it.'

It was weird, but I felt closer to Dad in that moment than I had for years. I didn't even feel scared, I just felt sad.

'*I* miss him too,' I said quietly. 'I know I was really young when he died, but I want to fill in the gaps in my memory. I want to know what he was good at and what he liked doing and what his favourite food was. I want to know everything.'

Dad didn't say anything for ages. He slumped back in his chair, resting his head on one side as if it was too heavy to hold up straight.

'I'll tell you one thing about him, Lizzie,' he said in the end. 'He loved *you*. I've never seen a teenage boy so soppy over his little sister.'

Dad probably didn't realize, but those few

words meant everything to me. Luke loved me. He was soppy over me. He must've held me and cuddled me when I was a baby, maybe he even helped Mum to change my nappies and feed me. It didn't solve the mystery of what happened to him in Spain, but it gave me the warmest feeling inside, like being wrapped in a soft blanket.

*　　　*　　　*

I was up and out of bed first thing on Wednesday morning—I couldn't wait to see Bee and to find out if she'd spoken to Aidan. I raced downstairs for breakfast, but I realized something was wrong as soon as I saw Dad. He was sitting at the table in his dressing gown, reading the paper, and it was already eight. He never came down for breakfast in his dressing gown on Wednesdays. *Never!* He always showered *before* breakfast so we could start our lessons early and he could get away to the office for his meeting.

'What's going on?' I said, from the doorway. 'Why aren't you dressed?'

He glanced up at me. 'What do you mean, Lizzie? It's only eight.'

'Yes, I know, but we always start lessons early on Wednesdays so you can get to the office.'

'I'm not going today,' he said, looking back down at the paper.

'But why not? Has your meeting been cancelled? You *always* go on Wednesdays. *Always!*'

He peered at me over the paper. 'Why the sudden interest?' he said, frowning, his eyes cold again. 'What difference does it make to you?'

'Nothing,' I mumbled. 'It doesn't matter. Where's Mum?'

'*She's* gone to the office to sort out some paperwork. She'll be back later this afternoon. Look, what's going on, Lizzie?'

'Nothing, really.'

I ran back upstairs and threw myself on my bed. How was I going to get out of the house now? How was I going to convince Dad to let me go to Dilan's for lunch? He was so strict about me seeing boys. Even if he said yes, he'd probably insist on coming with me or checking with Dilan's parents to make sure they were going to be in the house with us. Why had he picked this one Wednesday to miss his meeting? Was it just a terrible coincidence? Or had he found out, somehow, that I'd arranged to meet up with Bee?

Bee

I couldn't get the awful thought that Dad might be guilty out of my mind. He was missing, hiding away somewhere, I was sure of it. Not only that, but there was something wrong with his mobile. Every time I called him, it said '*Number not in use*' so I couldn't text him or leave him a message or anything.

I went over and over everything he'd said in the days leading up to the Friday he disappeared, to see if he'd mentioned anything or dropped any clues. It was easy enough to remember that we ate breakfast together or watched the same TV programme, but I'd been so focused on Melissa

171

Knight and the fact that it was almost the summer holidays that I hadn't really paid much attention to what he'd actually said.

I tried to imagine my dad as a murderer, but it was impossible to picture. My dad was the sort of person who hated arguments. He always went out of his way to try and keep the peace. If Mum was in a mood or wound up about something, he'd make her a cup of tea or rub her shoulders to calm her down. The only person he ever argued with was Aidan and even then it was Aidan who lost his temper, not Dad.

I've always been much closer to my dad than I have to Mum. When I was three, he gave up his job so he could stay at home to look after me. He'd take me to nursery and then, when I was five, to school. Pick me up and drop me off at all my play dates and after-school activities. We had so much fun together, it didn't seem to matter that Mum was always working or that Aidan was so moody and secretive.

Everything was fine until I started Glendale High. I can remember the day I found out I'd been offered a place. Dad said it was easily the proudest moment of his life. He picked me up from school, waving the letter about in the air as I came out of the gates, practically jumping up and down. We went straight to our favourite cafe and he ordered me the biggest milkshake with whipped cream and sprinkles on top.

I was happy enough at first; I loved the smart uniform and most of the teachers were okay. I didn't even mind the fact that we got so much homework. But when the bullying started, I didn't want Dad to know. I didn't want him to know how difficult I was finding it to make friends, how much I began to dread going in every morning. We never argued or fell out or anything—I just tried to avoid him so he wouldn't ask me too many difficult questions.

He was really upset, I could tell, and I hated the way we were drifting apart from each other, but it all became mixed up in my head until I'd convinced myself he'd be even more upset if he knew how unhappy I was. By the time he saw the tickets to Spain in the kitchen and disappeared, we were barely speaking. It was awful, but in the space of a year we'd gone from being really close to being more like strangers.

I hardly closed my eyes all night after getting that note from Lizzie. Dad had only been missing for three weeks but it was beginning to feel as if I'd never see him again. The next morning I stayed in bed until Mum left for work. It took a massive effort to get up, I was so tired, but as soon as I heard the front door close behind her I crept up to Dad's study, a tiny room at the top of the house. Nan was still asleep so I figured I had at least half an hour to search for clues. I had to find something to prove Dad was innocent.

I'd always loved Dad's study. There are maps and charts covering every centimetre of the walls and he's got these hand-painted models of the planets hanging from the ceiling. He was an astronomer before he gave up his job to look after me, and in the last year or so he'd been busy working on this new research project about the moon, and how it's slowly moving away from Earth.

He tried to talk to me about it once at dinner, to explain how the moon was moving away from Earth at the rate of 3.78 centimetres a year, about

173

the same speed as our fingernails grow. It stuck in my mind because I'd started to bite my nails soon after starting at Glendale and I remember glancing down at my hands and wondering if my poor, ragged nails would ever grow again.

It took a few moments for my eyes to adjust to the gloom. I was convinced any information would be hidden away in a drawer or on the bookshelves at the back of the room. Next to his desk there was a small metal filing cabinet with three deep drawers. I spent ages sifting through papers, shaking files to see if anything was hidden inside, keeping one ear out for Nan. I found a few letters and some emails he'd printed off, but they were all about his project.

And then, tucked away at the bottom of the last drawer, I found an envelope with Aidan's name written across the front but no address. My hands began to shake as I slipped a single sheet of paper out of the envelope. It was a short note, only three lines long. I grabbed the edge of the desk as my eyes ran over the words.

January 12th
Aidan, I know you're angry, I realize how you feel, but if only you could understand that we have to keep quiet for Bee's sake. If we spoke out now it would destroy her life. Haven't we all suffered enough already?
Dad

He'd written it in January, a few weeks after the terrible row they'd had on Christmas Day, but he'd obviously decided not to send it; either that or he didn't know Aidan's new address. I couldn't take it in. Why were they keeping quiet for *my* sake? And what was it they were keeping quiet about? I felt sick, a cold, hard lump settling in my stomach like a stone. Dad and Aidan were hiding something. Something BIG.

The row at Christmas had been awful. It was practically the last time I saw Aidan. Dad was trying much too hard, cracking jokes and being really fake and over-jolly, but the more he tried to get Aidan to join in, the more Aidan withdrew. Mum was fluttering about between the two of them, desperately trying to keep the peace, but in the end Aidan lost it.

He accused Dad of being selfish and cowardly; too scared to face up to the past. He went on and on, hurling accusation after accusation, and Dad just took it. He didn't try to defend himself or argue back, he just sat there with his shoulders hunched as the insults rained down on him. I begged Aidan to stop—I was in floods of tears— but he was beyond listening.

It was easily the worst Christmas Day ever. Aidan stormed out, Dad ended up in his office and Mum carried on serving up the turkey, desperately trying to pretend that everything was normal. I kept asking her where Aidan was and if he was coming back, but she just kept on nagging me to eat, piling food onto my plate, as if stuffing me with dried-out turkey would make everything okay.

Nan was the only one who seemed to realize how upset I was. She came into my room at bedtime and explained that Dad and Aidan were arguing about something that had happened a long time ago. She said all families row, especially at Christmas, and that they'd be friends again in no time. I remember going to sleep feeling so much better, but she was wrong about Dad and Aidan. They didn't make friends again. He'd only been round once since that day, to pick up his stuff—and he never called me or emailed or anything any more.

I'd been thinking about Aidan a lot since Lizzie told me about her brother; trying to remember the last time we spent any *proper* time together. It was weird but I didn't really know the first thing about his life. I didn't know if he had a girlfriend or where he worked. I didn't even know where he lived; not since he moved flats. I only knew that he was always angry, always ready to pick a fight, especially with Dad; but that was about it.

I stayed slumped against the desk, the note in my hand, desperately trying to understand what it could mean. Was I in danger? Did Dad disappear to protect me in some way? And what did that have to do with Aidan? I just didn't get it. I'd been searching for clues to clear Dad's name, to prove he was innocent, but now I was more confused than ever.

It was only as I was leaving the room that I noticed the calendar. It was pinned up on the wall behind Dad's desk, open at July. It was completely empty except for one day, which was circled in bright red marker pen. The date leaped out at me: JULY 31st. My heart started to beat so fast I thought it was going to burst out of my chest.

July 31st was the day before we left Spain to return home. It was the day Lizzie and her parents held the memorial for Luke. It was the anniversary of Luke's death.

Lizzie

I had to get out of the house. Dad was droning on about how certain types of energy can be transferred from one place to another, as if it was just an ordinary Wednesday morning, but if I didn't get to Dilan's house by twelve, Bee would think I didn't want to see her and I'd *never* find out what actually happened on the night Luke died.

I sat there watching Dad's lips move, but I had no idea what he was saying. I was completely trapped, a prisoner in my own home. Mum was still out so I couldn't even rope her in to distract him or persuade him to let me go. I glanced down at my watch. It was already half past eleven and he was still trying to drum the information into my head. Just thirty minutes left to plan my escape.

As soon as the lesson finished I slammed my books shut and ran up to my room. It was just gone twelve. Bee would already be at Dilan's house. She'd be waiting for me, wondering where I was. I went over to the window, pressing my face against the glass. It was so frustrating. I couldn't bear the fact that she was so close but so far away at the same time.

When Bee first told me about Melissa Knight bullying her, she said she felt scared all the time, that she wished she had the guts to stand up to her. We were sitting on our rock chatting and I remember saying that I'd sort Melissa out for her, that I wasn't scared of anyone. But it was such a lie. I'd never stood up to Dad, not properly. I might have answered him back sometimes or muttered under my breath, but that was as far as it went.

What would happen if I walked out of the house right now and went down the road to Dilan's? What was the worst thing that Dad could do? It was crazy, but just the thought of it made my stomach flip over, as if I was about to go on the scariest roller coaster ride. I sat on the edge of my bed, trying to tell myself it was no big deal, even though my legs had turned to jelly.

I was the coward, not Bee. She knew my dad thought her dad had murdered Luke, but she'd still gone round to Dilan's with that note for me, and she was obviously doing everything she could to find Aidan. I slipped her literacy book out from under my pillow. I could take it back to her right now, just get up and walk out of the house. Show Dad I wasn't scared of him, and show Bee how much our friendship really mattered to me.

The poems felt important suddenly, as if they were the only link I had left to Bee and our holiday in Spain. I opened the book and reread the poem she had written that last night about saying goodbye.

Goodbye
Pale face
Scared eyes
Deep fears
Hope dies
Tight hug
Something's wrong
Last shrug
Stay strong

Hot tears
Holiday's end
Take care
Best friend

My heart clenched up as if someone had reached into my chest and squeezed it. She'd totally captured that nightmare moment when Dad had dragged me away from her in the hotel lobby. I whispered the last two lines to myself: *Take care, Best friend*. Bee was the best friend I'd ever had. I didn't really know what her dad was guilty of, or why Aidan had written R.I.P. and that he was sorry on the back of the orange-peel photo, but it didn't matter. No one had the right to keep us apart.

I opened my bedroom door and listened. Dad was in the kitchen, making lunch. It was twenty past twelve. Any minute now he'd call me down. There was no time to mess about. I slipped off my shoes and crept down the hall towards the stairs, cursing every creak. I'd never noticed how hideously noisy the floorboards were before.

I stopped at the bottom of the stairs, pausing for a moment, pressing myself against the wall. The front door was only about five steps from where I was standing, but it was impossible to get there without being seen from the kitchen. I breathed in, trying to make myself as small as possible and then took the first step, my eyes fixed firmly on the doorway to the kitchen. If Dad came out, I'd just say I'd heard someone knocking on the door.

My hand reached for the lock, praying it wouldn't make too much noise. My heart was pounding. I'd never gone anywhere without telling Dad first. I eased the door open and slipped outside, closing it behind me as quietly as I could. Dad was standing at the stove, his back to the window. I felt guilty for a second, I don't know why. I was only going down the road to see my friend.

If my life had been normal I wouldn't have had to do this. I wouldn't have had to sneak out of my own house like a criminal. But it wasn't normal. There was nothing normal about it. I'd never been to school or been free to make my own friends, or popped into town to go shopping or see a film. Dad had tried so hard to keep me safe, but he'd only succeeded in driving me away.

I slipped on my shoes, crept past the kitchen window, and then a few steps later I began to run.

Bee

I got to Dilan's really early, way before twelve. It was warm out, but dull, the sun trapped behind a bank of clouds. I hung around outside his house, trying to keep my nerve. I'd told Bailey I wanted to come by myself so I could have a proper chat with Lizzie, but it wasn't just that. I didn't want to show him the note Dad had written to Aidan or explain why he had a calendar in his study with the date of Luke's death circled in red marker pen.

Dilan came out just after twelve. 'Is she here yet?' he asked as he came down the path. He looked really cool, in skinny black jeans and a black T-shirt. I wondered if he'd made an effort especially for Lizzie.

'Are you sure she said today at twelve?' I said, peering down the road.

'Positive. She said her dad was going to a meeting. She'd better come. She promised she'd tell me what was going on.'

I shot him a look, surprised. 'What do you mean? What was she going to tell you exactly?'

'I don't know, do I?' he said, shrugging. 'That's the whole point.'

We stood there in silence for a bit. A car cruised down the road towards us. I thought it might be Lizzie's dad on the way to his meeting but it was a woman with long, blonde hair and dark glasses. I looked at my watch. It was already ten past. What if she didn't come? What if her dad had found out? What if she thought *my* dad was guilty and she didn't want to be my friend any more? What if Dad *was* guilty and I never saw Lizzie again?

'She was really scared the other day, you know,' said Dilan after a bit. 'Maybe I should go and knock on the door. Make sure she's okay.'

'Are you serious? What would you say?'

'I don't know, just that we were expecting her for lunch or something...' He trailed off, scuffing the pavement with his foot. I stared at him. He must really like Lizzie if he was prepared to go round there again. I couldn't wait to tell her, if she ever showed up.

'She's probably just changed her mind about wanting to see me,' I said, my hand closing over Dad's note to Aidan in my pocket. 'I wouldn't bother if I was you.'

We stood there waiting until half past twelve.

Dilan tried his best to start up a conversation with me. He asked about school and then listed all his favourite bands, but I was much too wound up to chat. *She's not coming*, I kept saying inside my head. *She's not coming. She's not coming.* The road was deathly quiet. There was no one around; no one playing out, or mowing their lawns.

'Look, I'm going indoors,' said Dilan in the end, checking the time on his phone for the hundredth time. 'Give me a shout if she turns up.'

I nodded, tears stinging the corners of my eyes. 'Thanks anyway, you know, for taking the note and everything.'

I watched him go up the path and into the house. I think he felt bad for me. Or maybe he was just disappointed. I waited a few more minutes and then turned to go. Lizzie didn't want to see me again, it was so obvious. But then, just as I reached the corner of Cromwell Close, I heard someone shout my name. It was coming from behind me, from the direction of Lizzie's house. I swung round, my heart leaping, and there she was, tearing up the road, waving her arms about like a windmill.

'I'm here! I'm here! Don't go, Bee! I'm sorry I'm late!'

I started to laugh, forgetting everything else; I was just so relieved to see her.

'I thought you weren't coming,' I called out as she ran towards me. 'I thought you didn't want to be my friend.'

'Of course I want to be your friend!' She threw her arms round me, out of breath. 'I just had to sneak out without telling my dad—so don't be surprised if the police turn up at any moment!'

I glanced over her shoulder in the direction of

182

her house. 'But I thought Dilan said he was going to a meeting.'

'He was. He goes every single Wednesday. But can you believe he suddenly decided not to go today. I've no idea why. We should get out of here anyway, before he realizes I've disappeared.'

'Let's just tell Dilan you're okay. He was really upset you didn't show up.'

'Stop it!' she said, but her face turned crimson.

'Come on, it'll only take a second.' I pulled her through his gate and up the path. 'You're supposed to be having lunch together, remember.'

Dilan was the only one home. He said his parents were at work and his brother, Danesh, was doing some kind of summer school. 'I got the looks, he got the brains,' he joked.

'And the modesty!' Lizzie shot back, and he burst out laughing, slapping his hand on his leg as if it was the funniest thing he'd ever heard. We followed him into the kitchen and he grabbed a carton of orange juice out of the fridge. 'So are you going to tell me what's going on,' he said, 'or do you want me to start guessing?'

Lizzie shot me a look. 'I do want to tell you, Dilan, but it's really complicated, isn't it, Bee?'

I nodded, keeping my mouth shut. I didn't even know if Dilan knew Lizzie had an older brother who'd died. They were only three or four when they started having lessons together and seven when they stopped. For all I knew, he might think Lizzie had always been an only child.

'It's just that our families don't get on,' Lizzie explained. 'My dad really hates Bee's dad so he doesn't want the two of us to be friends. They're sworn enemies.'

Dilan opened his mouth to ask more questions, but just at that moment my phone rang. It was Bailey.

'I've found Aidan,' he said, without saying hello or anything. 'He messaged me back on Facebook. He wants you to go round there today at two. I've got the address and everything.'

'Oh my God! Okay, we'll meet you at the bus stop in ten minutes.' I closed my phone, my hand trembling suddenly. 'Bailey's found Aidan,' I said to Lizzie.

'No way.'

'We're going round there, now.'

'What, like *right* now?' She looked scared, her eyes huge in her face.

I nodded, pulling her towards the door. 'Come on, Bailey's waiting. He's got all the details.'

'But what about my dad?' said Lizzie, pulling her arm away. 'He doesn't know where I am.'

I stopped by the door. 'Well, I'm going to see him, even if you're not. I'm sorry, Lizzie, but I've got to find out what really happened to Luke.'

'Hang on, who's Luke?' said Dilan.

'My brother,' said Lizzie faintly.

I grabbed her again, desperate to get going, practically dragging her to the door.

'And who's Aidan?' Dilan called after us.

'*Mine*,' I called back. 'Luke was Lizzie's brother, and Aidan is mine.'

Lizzie

I let Bee pull me down the path, amazed at how confident and determined she was acting. It was only a few days since I'd last seen her, but she seemed different. The way she'd talked to Dilan, the way she was taking control…it was weird, as if we'd swapped roles.

'I can't just come round to Aidan's with you, not today,' I said, when we were out on the street. She was so focused on seeing him, I don't think she realized how scared I was. 'My dad will be freaking out right now, and the longer I'm gone the worse it's going to be.'

'But we really need to talk to Aidan. Can't you just text him?'

I shook my head. 'How can I? He's got my phone, Bee. He took it away when we got back from Spain.'

'Text him on mine then,' she shot back, holding her phone out to me. Our eyes locked.

She was challenging me. Daring me to stand up to Dad.

'You don't know what's he's like,' I said.

'I do,' said Bee quietly. 'He's a bully. And I know all about bullies.' Her eyes never left mine for a second.

The air around us was thick and heavy, pressing down on my chest, making it difficult to breathe. It wasn't like she was saying something I didn't know, it was just hearing her say it out loud. She was right. Dad was a bully. And he was SO controlling. A feeling of anger was bubbling

185

up inside me, fizzing round my body. He wanted to control every single aspect of my life. If I didn't stand up to him now, I never would.

I pushed her hand away. 'I'm not going to text him,' I said. 'That would be cowardly. I'm going to go home and tell him.' I knew I sounded braver than I felt, but it was as if the anger was speaking for me, giving me strength.

'Come on then,' said Bee, and she grabbed my hand again and started pulling me down the road towards my house.

'Wait, what are you doing?'

She glanced back at me, her face set in a determined frown. 'I'm coming with you, of course. I'm not letting you go through this alone.'

We ran down the road together, stopping outside my front door. I was hot and sweaty, my heart beating much too fast.

'You can do this, Lizzie,' said Bee. 'What's the worst thing that could happen?'

I didn't know but I was about to find out. The door swung open and Dad stood facing us, his arms folded across his chest.

'Get in the house, Lizzie.' His voice was low and menacing. He stood aside to let me pass, but I shook my head, too scared to speak.

'I mean it,' he growled. 'Get in. Now.'

'I'm g-g-going out with B-Bee,' I stammered. 'I just came back to tell you.'

'Did you now?' he said. 'How very thoughtful of you.' His voice was dripping with sarcasm, his face cold and blank, as if all his emotions were hidden behind an icy mask. Bee squeezed my hand. I squeezed back, so relieved that she was with me.

186

'I won't be late,' I said to Dad, feeling a bit braver. 'If you give me my phone back, I'll be able to text you.'

'Okay then,' he said slowly. 'Come inside and I'll get your phone. It's upstairs.'

'No, it's alright, I'll wait here.'

There was a long silence. He didn't know what to do. Not with Bee standing there.

'Get in,' he said in the end, his voice growing louder. 'I'm not discussing it any more, Lizzie. Just get in the house and we'll forget all about it. Say goodbye to your *friend* and that'll be the end of it.'

I shook my head again, taking a step back. 'I'm sorry, Dad, but I'm not coming in.' My eyes filled with tears suddenly. 'You can't keep me here like a prisoner just because Luke died. It's killing me.'

Bee gasped. My heart was beating so hard it seemed to fill my entire body. *Bang. Bang. Bang.* Dad's mask cracked. His face creased up, painful lines drawn deep into his skin. I couldn't stand it. I wanted to reach over to him and smooth them out. Delete what I'd said. Put the mask back in place.

'Come on,' said Bee quietly. 'Let's go.'

I backed out of the front garden, watching Dad the whole time. He looked smaller somehow, half his normal size. It was just like in Spain when I saw him crying in the woods. Ten years had passed since Luke died, but the way Dad was standing there on the doorstep, it was as if it had only happened yesterday.

I hardly spoke on the bus on the way to Bailey's house. I was scared if I said anything at all I'd start crying and I had a horrible feeling that once I started I wouldn't be able to stop. Bee talked non-stop, filling me in on what she'd been up to since I last saw her. She explained how Bailey had messaged every Aidan Brooks on Facebook and she showed me a note she'd found in her dad's office that her dad had written to Aidan. I read it two or three times but it didn't make sense.

'Don't worry, I don't get it either,' she said, folding it up and putting it back in her bag. 'I know it makes my dad sound guilty, as if he's hiding something. That's why I need to speak to Aidan.'

She was being so matter-of-fact; it was difficult to believe we were talking about Luke and the fact that her dad might be responsible for his death. I stared out of the window, trying not to think of Dad's face when I left him on the doorstep. I couldn't help feeling guilty, as if by choosing to walk away from him with Bee, I was somehow taking sides against my own family.

Bailey was waiting for us at the bus stop. He was much better-looking than Bee had described, like, seriously cute. His face lit up as the bus pulled in and he spotted Bee.

'Stay on the bus,' he called out, waving us back. 'Aidan lives right in the centre of town.'

He tapped his Oyster card and followed us up to the top deck of the bus.

'So tell me exactly what was in the message, word for word,' Bee said as soon as we were all sitting down. 'Did you print it off?'

'It was really short,' said Bailey. 'It just said something like, *Hi, it's Aidan, tell Bee I can see her today. I'll be home after two.* That was it apart from the address.' He reached into his pocket and pulled out a scrap of paper, waving it under her nose. 'He lives in that big block of flats near the cinema. Do you know where I mean?'

I didn't have a clue, but Bee nodded, her eyes wide. 'We're so close now,' she said, as if we were off on an adventure together. 'We're so close to finding out what really happened to Luke.' I wished I could share her determination—but no matter what we found out, Luke would still be dead and Dad would still do everything he could to stop me from living a normal life.

*   *   *

It was easy to find Aidan's flat. It was in the really tall block right on the edge of town. We were way too early, so we wandered round for a bit to pass the time. There wasn't really much to see, just a few shops, a cafe and a doctor's surgery. It wasn't the nicest place to live. There was something bleak and depressing about it, as if no one cared very much.

Aidan buzzed us in just after two and we took the lift up to the fifth floor.

'What's he like?' I said, turning to face Bee. I was already so churned up about Dad and what had happened earlier, and now I was about to come face-to-face with someone who actually *knew* Luke.

'I'm not really sure, to be honest,' said Bee. 'I know it sounds weird but I was only eight when he moved out and he doesn't come round much any more because of my dad. If I said they didn't get on, that would be like the understatement of the century.'

'I know, you told me on holiday. But do you think he'll mind that we've come with you?'

She looked away, blushing. 'I'm pretty certain he won't mind Bailey coming but I'm not sure how he'll react to you. I'm sorry, Lizzie, I don't mean that in a horrible way.'

'I know, don't worry. He'll probably freak out when he realizes who I am.'

The lift doors jolted open and Bailey led us down the corridor to flat 56. Aidan was waiting for us at the door, his arms folded across his chest. He looked just like Bee, with curly brown hair and tan skin. He started to smile, but then the smile seemed to fade away, as if he was trying to work out what was going on.

'We're here!' Bee announced, her voice much too loud in the quiet corridor. She sounded as nervous as I was feeling.

'Hi, Bee. Alright, Bailey?' said Aidan, standing back to let us in. 'You haven't changed much since I last saw you.' He smiled at Bailey and then his eyes slid over to me.

'This is my friend, Lizzie,' said Bee. 'She's Luke's sister.'

My heart started to beat faster. I'd had no idea she was going to blurt it out like that. I watched Aidan's face as he registered Bee's words.

'Luke who?' he said quietly. But it was obvious he knew. He was blushing. Big red patches spread over his face and neck.

'Luke, your friend who died in Spain,' I said. 'Luke who died ten years ago this summer.'

No one said anything. It was like I'd lit a firework right there in the entrance of Aidan's flat and this was the moment of silence before the

190

explosion.

'What the hell's going on, Bee?' said Aidan in the end. He sounded really angry. 'Why did you contact me through Bailey? Why didn't you just ask Mum for my number?'

Bee started to talk very fast. 'Look, I met Lizzie in Spain, on holiday, but now we're not allowed to see each other because Lizzie's dad thinks that our dad killed her brother, Luke. Not only that, but I can't ask Dad about it because he's gone missing. This letter came, addressed to Mum, and then there were loads of rows and then Dad disappeared. I thought he was staying at Uncle Ron's, that's what Mum said, but when I called Uncle Ron he said he hadn't seen Dad for ages.'

The whole story came tumbling out. I watched Aidan the whole time, but it was impossible to know what he was thinking.

'We had to come and see you because you were there,' I said, picking up the story. 'You were actually on that holiday in Spain when my brother died, so you *must* know what happened to him...' I trailed off, the words drying up in my mouth. It was so strange, talking about Luke in front of Bailey and Aidan, but we'd come too far to back down now.

'Look, I think you'd better all come in and sit down,' said Aidan. He looked scared. Tiny beads of sweat had appeared across his forehead. He led us into the lounge, waving in the direction of the couch. The room was a mess, loads of books piled up on the table, papers everywhere.

'I've just qualified as a science teacher,' he said to Bee. 'Well, chemistry, to be precise. Did Mum tell you?'

Bee shook her head, looking amazed, as if she didn't know the first thing about him.

'It was really tough,' he said. 'Hardest thing I've ever done. Would any of you like a drink? I'll stick the kettle on.' We all shook our heads, perching in a line on the edge of the couch.

'No thanks,' I said. 'We just want to talk. We want to know what really happened on the night Luke died.'

Aidan sat down opposite us, as if he was the head teacher and we were three naughty children who'd been called into his office. 'I wish I could help,' he said, not really meeting my eye. 'It was such a long time ago, you see...'

I glanced at Bee. She was staring at him, willing him to talk. She was as desperate as me to find out the truth.

'I didn't really know Luke, to be honest,' he went on, his voice flat and robotic, almost as if he'd rehearsed the lines. 'I mean, I remember the holiday, but Luke was older than me, we didn't hang out or anything. It was a terrible accident, that's what I heard.'

'But Mum said you were friends,' said Bee. 'She *told* me.'

'You know what Mum's like,' said Aidan, looking even more uncomfortable. 'Just because *she* was close friends with Suzie, Luke's mum, she liked to think we were all best mates. I hardly saw Luke that holiday.'

His eyes flickered towards me. It was so obvious he was talking rubbish. I stood up suddenly; I couldn't help it. How was I supposed to keep quiet when he was sitting there, lying to my face? I reached into my bag and pulled out the photo of me and Luke at the picnic. The photo of Luke with the orange-peel smile. The one with Aidan's message scrawled on the back.

'If you didn't know him,' I said, my voice shaking, 'if you weren't *mates*, how do you explain this?'

Bee

Aidan jumped up and snatched the photo out of Lizzie's hand, staring at it as if he couldn't believe his eyes.

'What's going on?' I said. 'What's in the picture?'

'It's me and Luke,' said Lizzie. 'But Aidan was there when it was taken. He's written a message to Luke on the back.'

'Look, you need to go,' said Aidan, his eyes darting towards the door. He looked nervous, as if he was worried someone was about to walk in.

'You did see Luke on that holiday, didn't you?' Lizzie went on, as if he hadn't spoken. 'You can't just throw us out and pretend you didn't know him. My brother died the day after that photo was taken and I want to know what happened.'

Aidan sank back down onto the sofa, still clutching the photo. 'Yes, of course I saw him,' he muttered. 'Luke was my best mate. I saw him every day. We did everything together.'

I couldn't believe it. 'But then why did you lie to Lizzie just now?' I said, beginning to get angry.

Bailey stood up suddenly. I'd almost forgotten he was there. 'I'm going to head home,' he said.

193

'You guys really need to sort this out between you.' He mouthed at me to text him. I nodded and then swung back round to face Aidan. He was still staring at the photo.

'Just tell us,' I said. 'Stop lying and tell us the truth. Why did you say you didn't know Luke if you were best friends?' I was so angry I wanted to shake him.

'I had to,' he said. His voice was tight. 'He made me.'

'What do you mean?' I glanced over at Lizzie and then back at Aidan. 'Who made you? You're not making any sense.'

'I didn't want to lie. I didn't want it to be a secret, but Dad made me. He said we had to keep it secret, but secrets eat away at you. They live inside you and poison everything you do.'

He started to cry. Big tears rolled down his face. He didn't even attempt to wipe them away. It was horrible to see him so upset; I couldn't bear it. But I couldn't bear for him to stop talking either. I went over and sat next to him on the couch.

'What was the secret, Aidan?' I said, desperate to find out now. 'What did Dad make you say?'

Aidan stared at the photo of Luke and Lizzie for the longest time, his face wet with tears.

'I'm sorry, mate,' he whispered.

'Sorry for what?' I said. 'You've got to tell us, Aidan. *Sorry for what?*'

He dragged his eyes away from the photo and we locked eyes.

'For killing Luke,' he said. 'It wasn't Dad who killed Luke. It was me.'

We all froze for a split second; no one moved or said anything. And then Aidan slumped forward in

194

the sofa, his head in his hands.

'Don't be stupid,' I said, pulling his hands away, forcing him to look at me. 'Luke died in a car accident.' I shook his arm hard, a rush of pure panic surging through me. 'I don't understand. You were only fourteen, Aidan. How could it be your fault? What are you talking about? How could *you* have caused a car accident?'

'Because Luke made me drive,' sobbed Aidan. 'He was out of control, drunk. I didn't want to drive the car, but he made me.'

I saw Lizzie stumble back, then lower herself onto a chair on the other side of the room. 'How did he make you?' I whispered. 'Tell us what happened, Aidan. *Please.*'

Aidan wiped his hands roughly across his eyes. 'It was the worst night of my life,' he said. 'I wanted to tell the truth straight away but Dad wouldn't let me. I know it sounds as if I'm blaming everyone else, but you weren't there, you don't know what it was like.'

He took a shaky breath. 'Luke was my best friend.' He looked over at Lizzie. 'We'd been friends for years, ever since our mums met each other at the baby clinic. We went to the same school, hung out at weekends, it was great. But then that year, the year he died, everything changed. Luke started to drink. He was skipping school, messing up big time. It's difficult to describe, but it was as if the Luke I knew had been replaced by someone else…'

He paused for a moment as if he was choosing his words carefully. 'He didn't want to come to Spain that year. He had a new girlfriend, Stacy; he was mad over her, but your dad said he was too young to stay at home by himself. He was hyped up from the minute we arrived, angry. He kept daring me to do things. Stupid things. Steal stuff from the tourist shops. Run across the road when cars were coming. Hide away in the caves with him, drinking...'

'In the caves?' I said. 'The caves on the beach? We were there... We found a carving on the wall. R.I.P...'

Aidan nodded. 'I did that. It was the day after he died. I didn't know what else to do. I couldn't talk to anyone or tell them what really happened.'

'What did really happen then?' I asked, anxious for him to carry on.

Aidan sighed heavily. 'The last night of the holiday—the night Luke died—things got out of hand. We'd been in the caves, drinking; beer mostly and a bottle of red wine. We'd both had far too much and that's when Luke came up with the idea of taking Dad's hire car. The parents were all out to dinner that night, with you two.' His eyes slid from me to Lizzie. It was so weird to think we'd both been there but had no memory of it.

'Our bedroom had a door leading into Mum and Dad's bedroom and Luke had noticed Dad's car keys in there when we'd gone in to see if there was any spare cash lying around for drink. He dragged me out of the caves and back to our hotel to get them. I wanted to say no, I knew it was stupid, but Luke just had this way of persuading me to do things. It was almost as if he had this weird power over me...' He trailed off.

'So what happened?' I said impatiently. 'You took the keys and then what?'

Aidan carried on, his voice shaking. 'Luke drove

196

the car first. It was scary as hell. He drove away from the hotel down this narrow, dusty street that led to the beach. I begged him to stop but he was enjoying himself too much. I tried to open the door but it was jammed or something and that's when I really started to panic. I was certain I was going to die.

'I told him I was going to text my dad. I waved my phone at him, but he didn't care, he was too far gone. I texted Dad to come and find me. My fingers were sweaty, slipping all over the phone. I told him where we were and that Luke was drunk and that I needed him to come and get me. I remember praying Luke would stop, that it would all be over, but he had other ideas. After a while of driving up and down, he said he wanted me to drive the car. He dared me.

'I said no way, I didn't want to. I knew it would be the stupidest thing I could ever do in my life, but he went on and on, goading me, calling me chicken, clucking like a hen. He said if I didn't drive the car we wouldn't be mates any more, but even worse than that, he said he'd tell Mum and Dad I'd been drinking and shoplifting and that it was my idea to take the car. All the stuff he'd been making me do.'

'He sounds horrible,' said Lizzie quietly.

Aidan shook his head. 'He wasn't horrible, he was drunk, but I was in such a state myself, I believed him. I said I'd only do it if he got out of the car to make sure no one was coming. I didn't want to get caught. I was so scared I'd get into trouble.'

He closed his eyes as if he'd been transported back to that night. As if he could see the whole scene being replayed.

197

'That's when it happened,' he whispered. 'Luke got out to keep watch. He stood directly in front of the car and waved me forward—he was jumping about, dancing almost. He gave me a thumbs up and then leaped out of the way, but I didn't know what I was doing and there was this roaring in my ears, as if my head was going to explode. I took my foot off the brake and the car lurched forward and then suddenly Luke was right in front of the windscreen again, banging on the car, yelling at me to stop, that someone was coming, but I slammed my foot on the accelerator instead of the brake. The car shot forward and hit him, knocking him backwards.'

It was like listening to the worst horror story. I glanced across at Lizzie but she had her eyes closed, as if she couldn't bear what she was hearing.

'It was terrible,' said Aidan. 'The car stalled and I sat there in shock, paralysed with fear. I couldn't move, or speak or anything...' He paused for a moment, taking a ragged breath.

'And then suddenly Dad was there, at the window, calling the ambulance, yelling instructions at me, and at some point during everything that followed, Dad told the police that he'd been driving and that Luke had jumped out in front of the car. He did it to save me. He lied for me. I was drunk, fourteen years old and I'd just killed someone.'

He started to cry again. I didn't know what to say. It was just too much to take in. Dad had lied to the police. That's why Lizzie's dad thought he killed Luke. I didn't dare look at Lizzie. I couldn't even imagine what she must be feeling.

'But didn't Dad get into trouble with the police?' I said in the end.

198

Aidan shook his head. 'There was an inquest, obviously, but Dad told the police that he'd driven down to the beach to pick me up, that I'd texted him. He showed them the text. He said Luke was drunk and that he'd jumped out in front of the car—that it was just a tragic accident.'

Lizzie stood up suddenly. 'But if everyone thought it was an accident, why does my dad hate your dad so much, that's what I don't get...'

Aidan shrugged, wiping his hands across his eyes again. 'He just couldn't accept that I was fine, not a scratch on me, but *his* son was dead.'

'And why do *you* hate Dad so much?' I said. 'That's what *I* don't get. It sounds as if he was doing everything he could to protect you. Keep you out of trouble.'

'I know he lied to save me, Bee, and at the time I was so relieved and grateful, but my best friend was dead and there was a part of me that wanted to own up and come clean about what really happened. I went along with the lie at first but I couldn't deal with it. Dad's never been able to understand how much I *needed* to tell the truth. It was like we had this dirty secret between us and it feels as if it's tarnished everything in my life.'

'I've got to go home,' said Lizzie. 'I've got to tell my dad. Tell him what really happened.' She snatched the photo back from Aidan and grabbed my arm. 'Come on, Bee. Let's go and tell him the truth together.'

'But it won't make any difference,' I said, pulling my arm free. 'He'll realize my dad lied on the night of Luke's death. That he's been lying for all these years. He'll go mad. It's not as if our families are going to become best friends all of a sudden, is it?'

199

'No, I know, but don't you get it, Bee? The accident was *Luke's* fault, not Aidan's or your dad's. It was *Luke's* fault. He forced Aidan to drive the car. We've got to make my dad realize that he can't just dump all the blame on your family.'

'But I don't want you to think it was Luke's fault,' cried Aidan. 'We were just kids. Your dad was really strict; you don't know what he was like. Luke was rebelling. He was just a normal teenager who went too far. We've all done stupid things, things we regret, but we don't expect to pay with our lives. I could tell you a million good things about him. A million reasons why he was the best friend I ever had...' Aidan trailed off, too upset to carry on.

'But that's why I've got to talk to my dad,' said Lizzie. 'I need him to see that Luke was just a normal teenager, and that I've got the right to be normal too. You can't stop me from telling him.' She grabbed my arm again. 'Come on, Bee. Let's go.'

She pulled me out of the room and towards the front door but as she reached for the handle the door swung open and a man stepped into the hall.

'No one's going anywhere,' he said, closing the door behind him.

It was Dad.

*   *   *

It felt like an eternity passed as I stared at Dad. Then I pushed past Lizzie and ran towards him. I don't think I'd ever been so happy to see someone in my life. He wrapped me in his arms and pulled me in close, holding me so tight it was difficult to

200

breathe, but I didn't want him to let go.

We stood there hugging for what seemed like an age.

'Hello, Bee, my love,' he said finally, pulling away slightly and looking down at me. 'You don't know how good it is to see you.'

'Where have you been?' I said. 'I've been so worried. I called Uncle Ron but he said he hadn't seen you for months.'

'He's been here,' said Aidan. 'Ever since the afternoon he went missing. He came here and he ended up staying.'

I swung round to stare at him. Aidan had just said himself that Dad had forced him to lie about the night Luke died, so why would Dad come here and why would Aidan let him stay?

'I don't understand,' I said, more confused than ever. 'I just don't get it.'

'Why don't we all sit down and talk things through?' said Dad. He looked over my head towards Lizzie. 'You must be Elizabeth,' he said, smiling warmly.

'It's Lizzie,' she whispered. 'Not Elizabeth. No one calls me Elizabeth any more.'

'She's my best friend,' I said into Dad's chest. 'We met each other in Spain.'

'I know,' he said. 'I've spoken to Mum. I know everything.'

He ushered us back into the living room and we sat down on the couch. I cuddled up as close as I could, scared he might disappear again. I didn't know how I ever could have thought he might be responsible for Luke's death. He could never hurt anyone. 'I still don't get why you're here,' I said. 'And why didn't you call me? I've been so worried.'

Dad's eyes filled with tears. 'I'm so sorry, Bee. I knew if I called you I'd have to tell you a whole pack of lies about where I was and what was going on. I just didn't know what to do for the best.'

'And what about Mum? Does she know you've been staying here?'

Aidan nudged Lizzie suddenly, before Dad could answer. 'Show my dad the photo of Luke, Lizzie. She knows about the accident,' he said, turning to Dad. 'I've told them exactly what happened on the night Luke died.'

Dad froze, his body rigid. 'You've *told* them?' he said weakly. 'How could you, Aidan? You promised. You *swore* you wouldn't say anything.'

'I know, Dad, I know I promised, but I'm sick of it! I've been lying for ten years and I just couldn't do it any more. Not after Lizzie showed me the photo.'

Lizzie held the photo out to show Dad. He took it from her, his hands trembling.

'Oh God,' he said. 'I remember that day. I remember everything about it.'

'Do you mean you were there as well? At the picnic?' said Lizzie.

He nodded. 'We were all there. It was the last time our two families were together. I'm so sorry, Lizzie,' he said, his eyes filling with tears. 'This must be so difficult for you.'

'I need to tell my dad what really happened,' she said. 'I need him to know that Luke made Aidan drive the car. I think deep down he knows that Luke was out of control, but he doesn't want to admit it to himself because he was partly to blame.'

'What do you mean?' said Dad, frowning. 'Your dad was still at the restaurant when the accident happened. How could he be to blame?'

'It's just that my dad was so strict and controlling—he still is—and Luke was rebelling against him. Aidan just told us himself that Luke didn't even want to come on holiday that year but Dad forced him. If my dad had let him stay in England, Luke would still be alive now. If he could just admit that to himself, he might change. He might be a proper dad again. Not angry all the time. He might even let me go to school, see Bee, normal stuff like that...'

Dad leaned across me and took hold of Lizzie's hand. 'It's not as simple as that,' he said gently. 'I want your dad to know the truth as much as you do, believe me, but you can't tell him.'

'Why?' said Lizzie. 'Why can't I?' She started to cry. It was awful. She was stuck in a strange place talking about her brother dying, hearing so many terrible things, and it was all so sad and hopeless. I moved away from Dad and cuddled up to her, whispering in her ear that I was sorry. I couldn't bear to see her so upset.

'Lizzie's right,' I said, turning to Dad. 'It's up to her if she wants to tell her dad.'

Dad shook his head. 'We have to keep on lying,' he said quietly. 'I'm sorry, Lizzie, but it's the only way I can protect my children.'

'*What do you mean?*' I said. 'I get why you need to protect Aidan, but why do you need to protect *me*?' I pulled the note from Dad's office out of my pocket. 'That's what you wrote here,' I said, reading it again, 'that you had to keep quiet for *my* sake, but I just don't understand why.'

Dad glanced at Aidan. 'If Lizzie tells her dad that Aidan was driving the car on the night of

203

Luke's accident and her dad goes to the police, there's a very good chance I'll go to prison. Perverting the course of justice is a very serious crime, Bee. I lied to the police that night, but I had to. I had to protect Aidan. And I have to keep on lying now to protect Aidan. He's just qualified as a teacher and if the truth came out it would be terrible for him. But I also have to protect you.'

I shook my head. *'But why?* I don't want you to go to prison, and I don't want anything bad to happen to Aidan, but what's it got to do with *me*?'

'Listen, Bee.' Dad sighed, pulling me close again. 'The day you won that scholarship to Glendale High, I was the proudest dad alive. But at the same time I knew the truth about Luke's death would have to stay hidden.'

I was totally stumped. 'You're not making any sense. What's Glendale got to do with any of this?'

'Think about it, Bee. If word got round that your dad was in trouble with the police, or in prison, it would be awful for you. Everyone would be talking about it, the pupils, the teachers, the *parents*. You know what it's like, Bee—girls at Glendale High don't have dads in prison. You'd be cast out, isolated—you'd probably have to leave. I couldn't let that happen.'

'But this is all twisted up and wrong,' I cried, getting up from the couch and facing Dad. I couldn't actually believe what I was hearing. 'I hate it at Glendale High. I'd be happy to leave tomorrow because I'm already bullied, every single day. I'm bullied for being clever and loving books and having a scholarship place, so how could things get any worse? If you told the truth I wouldn't be ashamed of you, I'd be proud—and I wouldn't care less what anyone else thought!'

They were all staring at me.

'I didn't know you were being bullied,' said Dad quietly. 'Why didn't you tell me?'

I shook my head. 'I didn't tell anyone. How could I? You were all so proud of me; you, Mum and Nan. I didn't want to let any of you down. Lizzie's the only person I've ever told. She understands what it's like to be bullied. She understands *me*.'

'Wait,' said Lizzie, 'maybe your dad's right. It's not as if telling the truth will bring Luke back, and you know what my dad's like. He'll go storming off to the police first chance he gets.'

'Yes, but it's not just Dad's decision,' said Aidan suddenly. 'Not any more.'

'What do you mean?' said Lizzie.

'Aidan means he's not going to live a lie for the rest of his life,' I said, glancing at him. 'It's not fair to force him to keep lying if he wants the truth to come out.'

Aidan stared at me, nodding slowly. 'I can't believe how much you've grown up, Bee,' he said.

My face grew hot. I couldn't believe it myself— but I'd changed over the summer. Everything had changed. 'There's still something I don't understand though,' I said to Dad. 'What was in the first letter? Why did it lead to so many rows between you and Mum?'

Dad glanced at Aidan again. They'd obviously discussed it. 'It was from Suzie, Lizzie's mum.'

'Yes I know, Nan told me. But what did it say?'

Dad looked down at his hands, sighing deeply. 'She was inviting us to Spain. She said she was holding a small ceremony to mark the tenth anniversary of Luke's death and she thought it was time to make a fresh start, put the accident behind us. I knew your mum would want to go and I panicked. I was scared that once we were there, one of them would blurt out the truth.'

'But why did you run off like that? Mum called the police and everything.'

Dad hesitated for a moment. He looked so worn out, dark shadows under his eyes. 'I didn't mean to disappear,' he said. 'I saw the tickets in the kitchen and I came straight round here to talk to Aidan, to warn him that your mum was going to Spain to see Suzie, and that there was a very good chance the truth would come out...'

'And?' It still didn't make sense.

'He was in the most terrible state,' said Aidan quietly. 'I'd never seen him like that. We started to talk, *really talk*, for the first time in years—since the accident really. And I began to understand how difficult it had been for Dad to keep the truth hidden. I began to see things from his point of view. To see how much he'd sacrificed just to keep me out of trouble.'

'It was such a relief to talk,' said Dad, 'after so many years of fighting.'

'Okay, I get that,' I said, 'but why did you stay here? Why didn't you come home, or ring to let us know where you were?'

Dad reached out for my hand. 'I just got this idea fixed in my head that if I disappeared your mum would realize how upset I was. It seemed like the only way to make her understand how crucial it was to carry on lying. I know how cowardly that sounds now, and I'm not proud of it, but Aidan could see how serious I was and he agreed to let

206

me stay, and more importantly, he agreed it was right to keep quiet.'

'Until now,' I said, dropping Dad's hand and standing up. 'I know it's a massive risk and that it might be awful for all of us, especially for you and Aidan, but it's time to stop lying, Dad. It's time for the truth to come out.'

Lizzie

I stared at Bee, amazed. I couldn't believe how brave she sounded and how sure of herself. She had that same determined look in her eyes that I'd seen on the bus. I tried to clear my mind, to decide what I should do next, but I was trembling all over. It was hearing Aidan describe the night Luke died. The way Luke forced Aidan to drive the car—threatened him—it made him sound like such a bully. And yet Aidan insisted Luke was the best friend he'd ever had. But why would you want to be friends with someone who treated you like that?

I stared at the photo of Luke with the orange-peel smile; my funny big brother—down on all fours with a slice of orange in his mouth, trying to make me laugh. It was like there were two Lukes: the lovely big-brother Luke and Luke the monster. 'There's still something I don't get,' I said to Aidan. 'If you took this photo the day before Luke died, how did it end up at our house, in Luke's bedside table?'

Aidan crossed the room to sit next to me on the couch. 'I came round,' he said. 'It was a

207

few weeks after we got back from Spain. I was wracked with guilt; it was literally tearing me apart. I wanted to tell your mum and dad the truth, explain what really happened. I wanted to give them the photo and tell them how sorry I was.'

I couldn't believe it. 'You actually went round to my house? After Luke died?'

Aidan nodded. 'Your mum answered the door but she was too scared to let me in. She said if your dad came home and found me there he'd go mad. She was in a terrible state, it was awful. She started to cry, really cry. I wasn't sure what to do. She became hysterical, sobbing and tearing at her hair. I knew I should leave but I couldn't move. In the end she ran into the downstairs toilet, shouting through the door that I should go, but I didn't go. I went up to Luke's room...' He paused, remembering.

'What happened? My dad didn't come home, did he?'

He shook his head. 'No, I didn't see your dad. I sat on Luke's bed for a bit and then I opened the drawer in his bedside table to find a pen, and I scribbled the message on the back of the photo. I felt close to him in his bedroom. It was the first time since the accident that I stopped shaking. I sat there for as long as I dared, and then, before I left, I slipped the photo in a study guide that happened to be in my bag and left it in his drawer. I know it sounds crazy but I just wanted him to know how sorry I was.'

We all sat there for a moment, lost in our own thoughts. Aidan was crying again. Silent tears trickled down his face. 'If only I'd refused to get in the car,' he said eventually, his voice a whisper. 'Or refused to take the keys in the first place. I go over and over what happened, but I always come back to the same point. We did take the keys and I did drive the car—and somehow, I killed Luke.'

'It wasn't anyone's fault, Aidan,' I said, standing up. 'You shouldn't blame yourself. I'm going home now,' I said, 'to tell my mum and dad.'

I walked straight out of the flat, without looking at Bee or her dad. I didn't want him to try and make me change my mind. I had no idea how Mum and Dad would react, but I had to tell them what really happened to Luke. It suddenly felt very important. As if the truth might finally set us all free.

* * *

As soon as I got off the bus I could feel my courage start to drain away. Dad would already be furious with me for running off with Bee. It had taken me so long to stand up to him, but I was still scared. The closer I got to home, the harder it became to put one foot in front of the other. My legs felt heavy, weighed down. Running off was one thing—but going back was something else altogether.

He was waiting for me in the kitchen. I could see him as I came up the path. Mum was standing next to him, peering anxiously through the window. My arm twitched by my side and I nearly waved, as if it was a normal day. But Dad's lips were set in a thin hard line, his mask firmly back in place. They were both at the front door before I could knock. Dad reached out to grab hold of me, but Mum pushed past him, wrapping me in her arms.

'What the hell do you think you were doing, going off like that?' Dad barked, trying to pull me away from Mum. I'd never seen him so angry; he looked as if he was about to explode.

'Leave her alone,' said Mum. 'Please, Michael, shouting isn't going to help.'

'Look, I need to talk to both of you,' I said, pulling back from Mum. 'Inside.'

Mum and I sat at the kitchen table. Dad stood by the door, glowering.

'What have you got to say for yourself then?' he said. 'This had better be good. We had all this nonsense with Luke. Going off without permission. Mixing with the wrong sort of people.'

'It's Luke I want to talk about,' I said, trying to hold my nerve. 'It's about the night he died.'

Mum's hand flew to her mouth.

'What the hell are you playing at, Lizzie?' snapped Dad. 'What could you possibly know about the night Luke died? You were a baby!'

I took hold of Mum's hand, rubbing it, leaning into her. 'I'm sorry,' I said. 'I know this is horrible for you, but I need to tell you what really happened.'

'What do you mean?' she whispered. 'What are you talking about?'

'It was Aidan who was driving the car that night, not Bee's dad,' I said, not daring to look at either of them. 'It was Aidan driving the car because Luke forced him to. I'm not making it up. Aidan told me himself.'

Mum squeezed my hand, her nails digging into

210

my palm. I could've stopped there, but I didn't. I told them the whole story. I told them Aidan was scared. That he didn't want to drive the car. I told them how Luke threatened him, forced him into an impossible situation. I told them about Bee's dad. How he found them because Aidan had texted him for help. Why he lied. How desperate he was to protect Aidan. And I told them about Aidan. About how desperate *he'd* been to tell the truth. How much he missed Luke, even now, after all these years. How he said Luke was the best friend he'd ever had.

Mum began to cry.

'I'm going to kill him!' said Dad, when I'd stopped talking. He was pacing round the kitchen, clenching and unclenching his fists. 'Lying for all these years. Protecting *his* son while *our* son was lying dead in the road. I'm going to tear him limb from limb.' He stormed out of the kitchen and then ran back in, grabbing his car keys.

'But, Dad, wait, don't you see?' I was desperate to make him understand. 'Bee's dad was just trying to protect his child, like you try to protect me. There's no difference, not really.'

'*No difference*,' hissed Dad, pushing his face close to mine. '*No difference? Are you out of your tiny little mind?*'

Mum leaped up. 'Stop it,' she said. 'You're not going anywhere. This ends right here.' She stood at the kitchen door, blocking his way.

'I'm warning you, Suzie. I'm going to kill that man and there's nothing you can do to stop me!'

I shrank back in my chair, fear clawing at my throat.

'No, Michael. STOP!' It was the first time I'd ever heard my mum shout. 'It's your temper that's got us here, not Aidan and certainly not Phillip. It's the way you throw your weight about, scaring me, scaring Lizzie, scaring poor Luke when he was a little boy.'

I stared at her, amazed. Her eyes were blazing, her face bright red. She was standing up to my dad, *finally*, after all these years.

'Just sit down,' she said firmly. 'Charging out of here in a state is only going to make things worse. If you want to blame anyone for Luke's death, you need to take a good hard look in the mirror.'

Dad took a step towards her, his face a mixture of fury and confusion. Mum had never spoken to him like that. I don't think anyone had ever spoken to him like that.

'Get out of my way, Suzie,' he said. 'Don't make me say it again.'

Mum shook her head. 'No.'

Dad hesitated for a moment as if he wasn't sure what he should do and then he let out a roar. It was like the cry of a wounded animal. I closed my eyes, a scream freezing on my lips. I wanted to get away from him, get away from that awful sound, but I was too frightened to move.

And then I heard something. Someone was banging on the front door. And a second later the bell rang.

Bee

We heard Lizzie's dad roar as we came up the garden path. I grabbed Dad's arm and pulled him towards the door, my heart racing. She must've told them.

'Quick, Dad, ring the bell,' I said, banging my fists against the door. 'Hurry up! We've got to save her.'

Dad rang the bell and we stood back. Everything went quiet, but it wasn't a good kind of quiet. Then something caught my eye through the kitchen window.

'Look, they're in there.' I dragged Dad towards the window. Lizzie was sitting on a chair with her knees tucked up and her arms over her head. Her mum was standing in the doorway and her dad was bent over, as if he was in pain. It was a horrible scene. They were all frozen but, even so, I could almost feel Lizzie's fear pouring off her in waves.

Dad leaned forward, over the flower beds, and banged his fist on the window. The reaction was instant, as if he'd brought them back to life. Lizzie's dad looked up, turning to face us, and in the same moment her mum slipped out of the room. Only Lizzie stayed frozen, her legs tucked up, her arms tight over her head. The front door swung open and Lizzie's mum stood there, breathing very fast, her face covered in a thin film of sweat.

'Suzie,' said Dad, pulling me back from the window and towards the door. 'Are you okay?'

'I'm fine,' she said, but she started to shake, tears rolling down her face. 'It's not me, it's Michael...'

213

'Hey, it's okay,' said Dad, reaching out to comfort her. 'We're here now.'

Lizzie's dad appeared behind them. I shrank back, trying to hide behind Dad.

Dad breathed deeply before he spoke. 'Michael. I know you're upset, but please hear us out. We just want to talk.'

Lizzie's dad stood there for a long time. I felt sad for him suddenly. It didn't matter how angry he got, he could never bring Luke back.

'You lied,' was all he said in the end.

'Yes,' said Dad. 'I lied to protect Aidan.'

'But what about Luke?' said Lizzie's dad, his voice breaking. 'What about my Luke?'

Dad took another deep breath. 'I'm sorry, Michael. I did what I had to do to protect Aidan.'

Lizzie's dad slumped against the door frame, as if all the fight had drained out of him.

'Come on,' said Dad firmly. 'We need to talk. It's something we should've done a long time ago.' He gave my shoulder a squeeze to reassure me and then walked past Suzie and into the house. My eyes stayed fixed on Lizzie's dad. He didn't move for a moment but then, with what seemed to take a monumental effort, he straightened up and followed Dad inside. Just at that moment Lizzie appeared from the kitchen, her face deathly pale. She stumbled towards me and collapsed into my arms.

'I told them what really happened,' she said into my hair. 'But I was so scared, Bee; I didn't know what my dad was going to do and then…it all sort of seemed too much for him, as if he couldn't bear it any more.'

I stroked her hair, holding her tight. 'You were

so brave, Lizzie, honestly. I can't believe you went through with it.'

'You made me brave,' she said. 'I couldn't have done it without you.'

We stood there hugging each other until Lizzie's mum came over and put her arms round both of us. 'Well done,' she said, squeezing tight. 'No more secrets and that's all down to you two.'

She went inside and Lizzie and I sat down on the doorstep to talk. We cuddled up close, going over everything that had happened since the last night of the holiday.

'Genius idea to swap the cases, by the way,' I said.

'Genius idea to go round to Dilan's,' she said back. 'I need to speak to him, actually,' she added shyly. 'I need to say thank you.'

'You do realize he's crazy about you,' I said. 'Like, head over heels.'

'Shut up,' she said. 'No he's not.' But her face broke into a smile for the first time all day.

Lizzie

It took me ages to stop shaking. I kept expecting Dad to storm out or do something terrible to Bee's dad. He'd said he was going to tear him limb from limb and now they were shut in a room together. I still wasn't sure if I'd done the right thing by bringing everything out into the open. Mum seemed okay about it, but Dad would never forgive Bee's dad for lying.

'Why is it taking them so long?' I said to Mum,

215

staring up at the kitchen clock. We'd come inside and she was fussing round us, making sure we had lots to eat and drink.

'It's been ten years, Lizzie, my love. They've got a lot of catching up to do. I thought we could try to put the past behind us this summer in Spain, but it didn't really work out.'

'My mum wanted to come to the ceremony,' said Bee. 'I'm sure she did. That's why we came to Spain in the first place.'

'I know, love, but she had a note delivered to our hotel on the first day of the holiday saying she couldn't go through with it. We were just checking in when this chubby man came over—he said he worked at the Bay of Caves. I sent a letter back the next day, saying I understood but that if she changed her mind she'd still be welcome, but I didn't hear anything, and then we bumped into each other in the market…'

'The second letter,' murmured Bee. 'The second pink envelope that I saw in Mum's bag.'

'I've got something to give you, actually,' I said to Mum, reaching for my bag. 'I found it in Luke's bedside drawer but it's actually from Aidan.' I took the orange-peel photo out and handed it to her.

'He said he came round just after Luke died,' explained Bee. 'I don't know if you remember. He was desperate to tell you how sorry he was.'

Mum nodded slowly, staring at the photo. 'Of course I remember,' she said quietly. 'But it was all so raw. I couldn't cope. I couldn't deal with Aidan's grief as well as my own.' She clutched the photo to her chest. 'Thank you,' she said. 'Please tell him I said thank you. It means so much.'

Bee and I were still sitting in the kitchen, talking, when our dads finally emerged from the front room. They looked completely wrung out, as if they'd both run a marathon.

'We're going round to see Aidan,' said Bee's dad. 'Bee and I dashed out and left him and he's been texting non-stop.'

Dad didn't say anything. He looked confused, as if he wasn't sure how he was supposed to behave. I couldn't believe he was going with Bee's dad to see Aidan. It was like a miracle. Mum went over to him and wrapped her arms round his neck.

'I'm so proud of you, Michael,' she said. 'So is Lizzie, aren't you, Lizzie?'

They sort of turned to face me and I nodded. I half wanted to get up and put my arms round Dad too. I wanted to trust him, but I was still scared he might flip.

I waited until they'd left for Aidan's flat and then told Mum I was going round to see Dilan. It was the weirdest feeling ever, to tell her I was going somewhere and then just walk out of the door. I felt like running, or flying even. I was free for the first time since Luke died.

Bee walked with me down to the end of the road.

'This probably sounds crazy after everything that's happened, but I hope you don't mind that I read some of your diary,' she said when we were standing outside Dilan's house.

'Don't be stupid, that was the whole point of swapping cases. And anyway, I read your poems: "The Friendship Rock" and the one about saying goodbye. They were amazing.'

Bee groaned, her face turning red.

'Don't be embarrassed!' I cried. 'I honestly don't think you realize how talented you are. I wish I could write like that. I'm still trying to write a poem about Luke...' I trailed off.

'I'll help you if you want,' said Bee. 'Maybe we could write it together.'

I gave her a big hug. 'I'd love you to help, but I really think it's something I've got to do by myself.'

She hugged me back and then skipped to the corner and stood there waving while I walked up the path to Dilan's. 'Have fun,' she called out. 'Let me know what happens!'

Dilan was home alone. He answered the door with headphones on and a can of Coke in his hand.

'Hi,' he said. 'How did it go?'

I nodded. 'Good, I think. Well, scary but good.'

We went into the kitchen and he grabbed another drink out of the fridge.

'I always knew you had a brother,' he said, opening the can and handing it to me. 'I just didn't remember his name, or anything about him.'

'He died when I was really young. It was before we ever started our lessons together. There are photos of him all over the house.'

'Yeah, I know, but it was such a long time ago. I do remember sliding down the stairs in your duvet cover though, and making that dragon.'

'*No way!*'

He nodded, half-blushing, half-grinning. We stood there awkwardly for a minute.

'I just came round to say thank you, really,' I

218

said, to break the silence. 'For dropping Bee's note round and stuff...'

'Hey, what are neighbours for?' he said. 'Does your dad know you're here, by the way? He's not going to burst in and attack me or anything, is he?'

'Don't be stupid. He's out. With Bee's dad.'

'Phew, that's a relief,' he said, pretending to wipe sweat off his forehead. 'You can come round any time, every day if you like, as long as it doesn't put my life in danger!'

I smiled, my heart racing a million miles a minute.

'Oh, I think you'll survive,' I said.

Bee

I couldn't wait to get home. I couldn't wait to see Mum's face when I told her that Dad was over at Aidan's flat, *with* Lizzie's dad, and that everyone knew the truth. It took ages for the bus to come; it felt like hours. I leaped off at the other end and raced all the way home. Mum was in the kitchen with Nan and it was obvious from the second I stepped through the door that they already knew.

'Dad just called me!' she cried, as I burst in. 'I just don't believe it. Dad and Michael over at Aidan's! I can't get over it. And it sounds as if it was all down to you and Lizzie!'

I stood at the door, grinning. It was brilliant to see her looking so happy, but there was still so much I needed to understand. 'Did you know all along that it was Aidan who was driving the car?'

I said, going over to sit with them. 'Did you know about Dad making him lie?'

Mum's face fell. 'Not at first,' she said quietly. 'Dad told me just after we got home from Spain. I was furious to start with. I knew it was wrong. It wasn't just that we were lying to the police, it was the fact that we were lying to Suzie and Michael.'

'What happened?'

'I nearly went to the police,' said Mum. 'I was all set to go the following morning, but that night Aidan woke up screaming. I rushed into his room to comfort him and he clung onto me, sobbing. He was so young, so vulnerable. I rocked him in my arms like a baby until he calmed down and I knew at that moment that I couldn't bring myself to turn him in. I'm not proud of it, Bee, but he was still my little boy, and it just felt as if his life would be over before it had even started.'

We were all quiet for a moment, thinking of Luke, and how *his* life *was* over before it had really started.

'He was a good boy, Aidan,' said Nan quietly. 'He was just scared of losing Luke's friendship, that's why he went along with everything. But even so, it's always better to tell the truth.'

Mum nodded, agreeing. 'I realized that very quickly, so did Aidan. He was desperate to reveal what had really happened. It started to have an effect on all of us in different ways. Dad couldn't concentrate on work. He had these awful nightmares and flashbacks. So did Aidan. He was a mess. They were both struggling to come to terms with what had happened, but it was as if sharing the secret drove them apart. Their relationship was in tatters, but Dad was still convinced that telling the truth would ruin Aidan's life. And then, more recently, he became convinced it would ruin yours.'

'I think it's ruined Aidan's life anyway,' I said. 'And Lizzie's.'

'That's why I was so desperate to go to Spain,' said Mum. 'To try to put things right.'

'But Lizzie's mum said you had a note delivered, the day we all arrived...'

'I know. I sent it with Carlos. I realized the second the plane landed that I couldn't face them. I just felt so guilty about covering up the truth. Every time I thought about seeing Suzie, my throat started to close up. I wanted to be brave, but then Carlos made that comment about it being paella night and I remembered that the night Luke died it was paella night as well—we'd all been at the hotel restaurant having such a wonderful time... It was the last time we were together.'

'So you told Suzie you didn't want to come to the ceremony and then you saw her in the market...'

Mum nodded, her eyes glistening. 'We were such good friends, Bee, and I'd missed her so much, and just seeing her like that, after so many years, it was so difficult... Oh God, I can't wait to call her, to see her properly...'

We were still talking things through, making sense of everything, when Bailey texted me. I left Mum and Nan in the kitchen and went next door.

'I've been going mad,' he said when I got there. 'What happened after I left?'

'Well, it turns out it was Aidan who was driving the car the night Luke died, not my dad. They were drunk and Luke was threatening him.'

'You're kidding! And then what?'

'It's too long to go into properly but Lizzie told

221

her parents what really happened that night. Her dad went completely ape and then he calmed down and now they've gone to see Aidan. My dad and Lizzie's dad round at Aidan's *together.*'

'No way!' said Bailey, shaking his head, his fringe flopping down over his eyes.

My heart suddenly started to beat very fast. I didn't care any more that he was Bailey my next-door neighbour, Bailey my old friend and almost brother. 'Yes way,' I said. 'And there's one more thing. Thank you for helping me find Aidan and for being so completely brilliant.' I leaned up and, before I could change my mind, I kissed him, right on the lips. And then I turned and ran back through the front door.

'Blimey, Bee!' he called out after me.

But when I glanced back, he was leaning against the door frame, grinning.

Lizzie

I wrote the poem for Luke later that evening. After struggling to write a word for weeks, it was amazing how easily it came to me. It was the photo. The picture of Luke, down on all fours with the orange peel in his mouth. There was something about that image of him that told me everything I needed to know about my big brother.

When I finished the poem I copied it out really neatly and went downstairs. Mum and Dad were in the lounge, talking quietly. Dad looked different, older. I wanted to go to him, to tell him I

222

loved him, but I still felt scared.

'I think we should have another ceremony for Luke,' I said. 'I've written a poem and I'd really like to read it out.'

Mum's face broke into a smile. 'Oh, that's a lovely idea, Lizzie.'

'But I want Bee to come,' I added, before I could lose my nerve. 'And her mum and dad, and Aidan. Is that okay?'

Dad flinched slightly, but he nodded.

'Nothing over the top or fancy,' said Mum. 'Just our two families together.'

*   *   *

We held the ceremony a few weeks later, just before the end of the summer holidays. Mum and I went to the garden centre and bought an orange tree. Mum was so happy I wanted to do something for Luke, I think she would've bought me a whole orchard of orange trees if I'd asked. She said she felt as if a weight had been lifted off her heart for the first time in ten years, and that Dad felt the same, even if he found it harder to say.

'Losing Luke nearly tore us apart. Dad was filled with so much anger and guilt, but most of it was directed at himself and he just didn't know how to deal with that. That's why he lashed out all the time. I'm not making excuses for him, Lizzie, I just want you to understand. It wasn't anything you did wrong.'

'I know, Mum,' I said. 'I do understand.'

Bee and her family came over in the afternoon. It was lovely having them in the house, much

223

less stressful than I'd imagined. Mum and Suzie couldn't stop talking. They nattered away in the kitchen, bringing in plates of sandwiches and cakes, laughing one minute, crying the next. It was so nice to see them together. It just felt right.

First chance I got, I took Bee up to my room and told her about Dilan. I'd only seen him once since everything happened—he came over one morning and we just sat in the garden, chatting. I had to pinch myself a few times to make sure he was really there and that Dad was cool about it.

'I told you he was crazy about you,' said Bee. 'It was so obvious that day we were round at his; the way he laughed at your jokes.'

'What do you mean?' I said, pretending to be offended. 'My jokes are really funny! Anyway, how about you and Bailey?'

Bee shrugged, turning beetroot.

'What? What's going on?'

She covered her face with her hands. 'I kissed him,' she whispered through her fingers. 'On the lips.'

My mouth fell open. 'You *are* kidding me!'

'I'm not, but I'm so embarrassed about it, you wouldn't believe.'

'And have you seen him since then?'

'Yeah, I've seen him, but neither of us mentioned it. It's like the biggest nightmare.'

I grabbed my pillow and pretended to kiss it, singing, 'Bee and Bailey sitting in a tree— K.I.S.S.I.N.G!' Bee tried to grab it back, but I rolled away, kissing the pillow over and over and laughing so much I couldn't breathe. She jumped on top of me, wrestling the pillow out of my arms, tickling me all over, until we were lying next to

224

each other, out of breath, tears streaming down our faces.

'You're so horrible,' she gasped. 'I should've ignored you that first day I saw you sitting up on your rock. I should've walked straight past without stopping.'

'You couldn't,' I said, serious for a moment. 'We were destined to meet each other again. And destined to be best friends.'

We lay back, staring up at the ceiling.

'Best friends for ever, right,' she said, linking her little finger round mine.

'Right,' I said, smiling. 'Best friends for ever.'

*   *   *

I read my poem out after tea. We went into the garden and planted the orange tree in a big ceramic pot and then stood in a circle round it: me, Bee, Mum, Suzie, my dad, Bee's dad and Aidan. We didn't hold hands or anything, but the circle felt strong—and standing there, in the warm afternoon sunshine, I felt safe for the first time in years.

Bee had brought a red balloon. She said she wanted to release it into the air as a special way of saying goodbye to Luke. We watched it float up over the garden fence, reaching for the clouds, as I began to read.

'My Orange-Peel Brother,' I whispered, my voice shaking slightly. 'This is for you.

I've been trying to find the brother I lost
Through years of lies and fear and shame

225

The times I've wondered if I was to blame
For staying alive when he was dead
For all the things that were left unsaid
For not feeling sad or missing him much
Or knowing his voice; remembering his
    touch.

I've been trying to find the brother I lost
Using the clues to track him down
The brother who liked to act the clown
Down on all-fours, mucking around
The brother who made me laugh and clap
I've been following the clues, using the map
To find my brother as fast as I can
The lies disperse like grains of sand.

My orange-peel brother who's so far away
So hard to reach when I'm desperate to say
I love you and miss you and wish you were
    here
Close by my side to blot out the fear
My orange-peel brother, the tears that
    we've cried
You were tough on the outside, but sweet
    inside
I'll love you for ever, my orange-peel
    brother
I'll love you for ever more.'

Bee

My eyes snapped open. I looked at the clock. 6.30 a.m. It felt as if this moment had been creeping up on me all summer. My first day back at Glendale High.

I hadn't really thought about Melissa Knight since we got back from Spain—there'd been so much else going on—but Mum and Dad had sat me down last week for a long talk about the bullying. Aidan was there as well, and Nan. We'd just had Sunday lunch together—a proper family meal with no rows or upsets.

'We don't mind at all if you want to change schools,' said Mum when I'd finished telling them everything. 'Blow the scholarship! We just want you to be happy.'

'I know, and I have thought about changing, but that would be like running away—and if I've learned one thing this summer, it's that running away doesn't solve anything.'

'Quite right,' said Nan, nodding.

'But are you sure you can deal with it? Deal with this girl, Melissa?' said Aidan. 'It sounds as if you've had an awful time.'

'Of course I can deal with it,' I said, jutting my chin out. 'You have to stand up to bullies. Show them you're not scared.'

Dad shook his head. 'I just don't know when you got to be so wise and so brave,' he said. 'I'm so proud of you, Bee, you've got no idea.'

And I had felt brave, last week, when we'd had that conversation. Well, determined to stand up to

227

her anyway. But now the actual day had arrived, I wasn't so sure. I picked at my breakfast, watching the clock as it sped towards 7.30. If I was going to catch the bus I had to get going. Mum offered to come with me; she said she'd drop me off on her way to work, but I shook my head.

'I'm fine,' I said. 'If you take me they'll know I'm scared.'

I hauled my bag onto my back and left for the bus stop, telling myself to be brave with every step I took. Lizzie thought I was brave. She said I was the bravest person she'd ever met. I held onto that thought as the bus pulled in and I climbed the stairs to the top deck. Lizzie would probably have swapped places with me in a flash too. The last time I'd spoken to her she was still trying to persuade her dad to ditch the homeschooling and let her start proper school.

The bus stopped right near Cromwell Road, two streets away from Lizzie's. I felt as if there was a brick in my stomach. I got off and then stood at the bus stop for a moment, before forcing myself to join the stream of girls walking in the direction of the school. I wasn't 'Bookworm Bee' or 'Brainiac Bee' any more, I was 'Brave Bee', and no one was going to push me around or put me down.

'Hey, Bee!'

Someone was calling me.

'Slow down!'

My heart stopped. I turned round, expecting to see Melissa Knight or one of her stupid mates. I blinked in the September sunshine and then blinked again, convinced I must be hallucinating. It was Lizzie, running towards me. And she was wearing a Glendale High uniform!

She flew into my arms, laughing. 'Oh my God! I nearly missed you! I've been so excited. I've actually known for about two weeks but I wanted it to be a surprise!'

I pulled away from her. 'Known about what? What's going on, Lizzie? What are you doing here?'

'I'm coming to Glendale High!' she cried. 'I wore my dad down. I just went on and on about how it was practically at the end of the road, and that it was a really good school and that I already had a best friend there and in the end I think he just agreed to shut me up. Can you believe it? Isn't it amazing!' She barely paused for breath. 'We went up to meet the head the other day and I had to sit a test, but that was fine, especially the literacy, and then Mum took me to get my uniform from the special store in town, and here I am!'

I shook my head, completely speechless. I just couldn't believe it. Lizzie at Glendale High. The best friend I'd wished for, that first day on the beach.

'Come on, Bee!' cried Lizzie, linking arms with me, and pulling me down the road. 'Let's go get Melissa Knight!'

'Melissa *who*?' I said, and we looked at each other and burst out laughing.